**DO NOT REMOVE
CARDS FROM POCKET**

FICTION
WARNER, MIGNON. 2198236
DEVIL'S KNELL /

OCT 27 '83

DEVIL'S KNELL

BY MIGNON WARNER

Mignon Warner

DEVIL'S KNELL

PUBLISHED FOR THE CRIME CLUB BY

Doubleday & Company, Inc.
Garden City, New York
1983

All of the characters in this book are fictitious,
and any resemblance to actual persons,
living or dead,
is purely coincidental.

Library of Congress Cataloging in Publication Data
Warner, Mignon.
Devil's Knell.
I. Title.
PR6073.A7275D48   1983   823'.914
ISBN 0-385-18922-2
Library of Congress Catalog Card Number 83-45016

First Edition

DEVIL'S KNELL

CHAPTER 1

The electric clock on the wall click-clicked, hummed, then click-click-clicked again. For the moment, it was the only sound in the post-office section of the village store where the modern clock was located. There was a Victorian railway clock mounted on one of the tiled pillars in the store, but it had given up the ghost along with old Miss Dunphie. (This wasn't strictly true, but it was the kind of colourful folklore newcomers to the village expected to be regaled with, and so the story had persisted over the years with no one now doubting its veracity.) Certainly, no amount of *in situ* do-it-yourself repair on the antique clock done since the old postmistress had passed on would prevail upon it to start up again. Miss Holliday, the present postmistress and former counter assistant to whom Agatha Dunphie had left everything—the post-office stores and Rose Cottage—said she couldn't get the clock down from the pillar when someone suggested that she should take it along to a proper clock repairer in Gidding. But this was widely thought to be an excuse not to do anything about the matter. Miss Holliday had a reputation for being close with money. Hardly a day went by that someone in the village did not find some reason for declaring that she probably still had the first penny Agatha Dunphie had ever paid her.

The post-office clock hummed and buzzed like an irritable wasp, and Miss Holliday looked up from the column of figures she had been trying to add up and frowned at it. She was perched on a tall stool, with her back to the main post-office counter. The clock was on the whitewashed rear brick wall of the post office, directly over the narrow, high counter on which she was working. She didn't like clocks. Not the ticking kind with big faces like old Miss Dunphie's railway clock. This was really why she didn't want it repaired. She had offered it to Arthur, Miss Dunphie's nephew (the executors had told Miss Holliday that she wasn't obliged to, but it would be a nice gesture if she were to offer the young man something from his late aunt's estate, seeing as how the old lady hadn't left him anything), but Arthur had simply looked Miss Holliday up and down scornfully and said that if a useless, broken-down old woodworm-infested clock was the best she could do, then she could forget it.

The electric clock clicked, whirred, then settled down peacefully again. Miss Holliday tried once more to add up the column of figures, but it was hopeless. She couldn't concentrate her mind on anything this morning. Time was running out, and, she thought with a cross frown, it was almost as though that wretched clock on the wall knew it and was determined not to give her any peace until she had made up her mind what she was going to do.

She took off her tinted spectacles, then momentarily closed her eyes and put her hand to the bridge of her nose, stroked it thoughtfully. The sensible thing to do when Mr. Smith proposed to her was to refuse him. (No doubt about it, he *was* going to ask her to marry him; he was on the point of asking her last Sunday afternoon, only she had managed to forestall him.) If she said no, her life would simply go on as always, quietly and smoothly, with nobody knowing the truth until she died. Perhaps not even then. They would simply think that all the documents—the papers which proved people were who they claimed to be—had become mislaid or lost, accidentally destroyed. That sort of thing must happen often to lots of perfectly respectable people. . . .

She quickly covered her eyes with her hand. She had come over giddy, a little breathless. The thought of saying no to Mr. Smith overwhelmed her. She was so tired of being sensible. Sometimes it seemed as though this was all she had ever been —interminably deadly dull and sensible, *careful*, with no ups and no downs. In point of fact, this was how she saw her life, as one long, straight line like that on the monitor of a life support machine when the critically ill patient connected to it has died. She had a strange feeling sometimes that she wasn't really here, that someone, somewhere, a long while ago, had switched her off.

She took a very deep breath, held on to it. She could stand another week, another month, six months, if necessary, of this boring, humdrum existence. But a whole lifetime of it? Slowly, she exhaled. She was no Agatha Dunphie. She knew it, and so did they, the villagers. They had just about reached an impasse. They couldn't take much more of her, and she definitely couldn't take much more of them. The pensioners were the worst. How she loathed them for their whining and carping, the selfish demands they made on her. They were like spoilt children. . . .

Tilly Cockburn, the cheerful middle-aged woman who managed the grocery store for Miss Holliday, her plump hips swelling up and down under her too tight, blue-check overall, suddenly came out of the side stock-room with a long wooden pole, on the tip of which was a small metal hook for lowering high window-sashes. Tilly went outside and used the pole to unhook and lower the red-and-white-striped sun-blind. The hot, late May sunshine was already slanting across a corner of the wide plate-glass store-front and would, before long, be beating directly against it and heating up the cluttered interior of the small store, making working conditions most unpleasant.

Miss Holliday watched Tilly for a few moments, then put on her spectacles and looked back at her work. A fly was crawling lethargically up the column of figures, pausing every now and then as if actually adding them up as it progressed up the page.

Absently, Miss Holliday watched it. . . .

Everyone was sure to whisper and make snide remarks: they'd all say she and Mr. Smith were not suited to one another. Not one of them would really understand. Companionship: that was what she wanted, what they both wanted. Not the other thing. Sex. Arthur said she was frigid. But that wasn't true, Miss Holliday thought with a tiny frown. She simply wasn't interested. She'd never been interested. A look of annoyance crossed her face. Why did everything have to be given labels like this, categorised? *Frigid.* Her thin, drooping lips formed the word, but she didn't say it out loud. It sounded so freakish. Old-maidish. She scowled darkly. Who could honestly define what was normal where sex was concerned? If the truth were to be known, she was probably more normal than most. A darn sight more honest, that was for sure. It was the pot calling the kettle black where Arthur Dunphie was concerned, anyway. What about his hang-ups? She'd dearly love to know what a psychologist would make of the number of times Arthur used the word "luck" when in conversation with someone. He was obsessed with it. Equated every single thing that happened to him in terms of luck, good or bad, depending on the circumstances.

But this wasn't solving anything.

What on earth was she going to do?

For some people, she thought peevishly, the solution would be simple. They would forget about the formal paperwork and simply live together. But with Mr. Smith's kind of job, this was right out of the question. The Church wouldn't wear it, and somehow she didn't think Mr. Smith would either. And anyway, she thought with another irritable scowl, it was only prolonging the inevitable. Even if Mr. Smith were in a position where they could ignore what everyone thought and set up house together, there would be all those holiday trips abroad he kept talking about. An application for a passport to be made. Official forms to be filled in. . . .

Two young mothers, one in an ethnic skirt and blouse and the other in a canary-yellow T-shirt and jeans and with their small offspring in push-chairs, suddenly filled the half-open doorway. They didn't come right into the store. They remained outside discussing the respective family holidays they planned to take in summer in relation to the continuing fine weather, abruptly pausing and breaking briefly apart from one another a minute or so later to let Tilly by. One called out to Tilly, jocularly surmising that business must be really bad if she, Tilly, had to resort to prowling up and down the front of the store with a hooked stick to snare a customer. Tilly grinned and made a playful move in the young mothers' direction with the window-pole, then continued on to the stock-room.

The two young women went on talking about the weather, which had been hot and muggy for over a week now, and speculating on what Stan North—a villager like themselves— had said on television the previous night. Spring had been bitterly cold and wet, and as was often the case when there was any deviation in what were considered "normal" weather conditions, Stan North, who kept weather records for a hobby (and, it was claimed, got his inside information from sitting motionless in the hedgerows for hours on end monitoring the behaviour of the insect life which abounded in such places), was summoned into the local television centre to give his opinion on the wet spring. He said it pointed to a long, hot summer, and he had all the facts and figures going back over many years to back up his claim.

"Poppycock," muttered Miss Margaret Sayer, who caught snatches of the young women's conversation as they moved swiftly aside to permit her to enter the post-office stores. The diminutive, seventy-four-year-old spinster headed straight for the post-office counter on the far side of the store. "Never heard such a load of old codswallop!" she snorted at a large jar of brown-and-white-striped humbugs.

The two women in the doorway grinned slyly at one another and continued with their conversation. They were actually quite relieved that they had got off so lightly, and as both had neglected to put cotton hats on their toddlers' virtually hairless heads (one of Miss Sayer's pet summer-time hates), they prudently moved on out of the firing line. The old battleaxe was sure to have a go at them on her way out about the dangers of sunstroke and the irresponsibility of young mothers today and how different things were when she was their age. And so on and so forth.

Miss Sayer glowered through the barred post-office window.

Miss Holliday was still sitting on the stool with her back to her customers. Miss Sayer shuffled her size-two feet impatiently on the worn brown-and-gold mosaic-patterned linoleum floor-covering, but to no avail. The postmistress took no notice of her.

At last finished with her column of figures, Miss Holliday unhurriedly secured the sheet on a clipboard, then opened a deep drawer to her right and began to sort through the morning's registered mail.

Miss Sayer began to fume. She slapped her pension book loudly on the counter.

The postmistress glanced round imperturbably at her and went on with what she was doing. "It's half-day closing today, Miss Sayer," she reminded her irate customer. "I'm on my own this morning. You'll just have to be patient and wait, or come back a little later on." She inclined her head at the wall clock, which showed twelve minutes to midday. "The postman will be here to collect the mail in a few minutes, and I can't keep him hanging about waiting while I get everything sorted out."

Miss Sayer was livid. But she made no reply. Miss Holliday was one of the few people who invariably proved a match for her. Miss Holliday was a match for most people, with the exception of a handful of very young children who hadn't yet reached the age of reason and good common sense. The village academics, headed by Frederick Linthorpe, a retired English professor and a recognised authority on British folk customs, had dubbed Miss Holliday Little Gidding's *bête noire*. But this was far too subtle for the more prosaic villager who commonly referred to Miss Holliday as "Her in post office," but in such a way as to conjure up visions of someone far more terrible than the professor's "black beast." Miss Holliday was universally disliked. Everyone had a tale to tell about the woman, some personal grievance held against her. She was the village bully, someone once said of her. She terrorised everyone without lifting a finger against a living soul.

There were a lot of reasons put forward for her crabbiness. (Miss Holliday had no contact whatsoever with anyone in the village outside normal trading hours, and all grievances were therefore strictly business-related.) The most popular theory was predictable: she was a frustrated old maid. But at thirty-four—or thereabouts; no one was too certain, not even Tilly, who probably knew her better than anybody, including Arthur Dunphie—she surely had a few years yet ahead of her before she could justifiably be termed "old." And the explanation which perhaps came nearest to the truth: she was plain bad-tempered, what was vulgarly known as "a nasty bit of work."

A petition to the Head Postmaster in Gidding, signed by over eighty per cent of the villagers, insisting that she be replaced, had been rejoined with the unpleasant news that if and when Miss Holliday gave up her post, it was planned to close down the sub-post office in Little Gidding, and thereafter, the villagers would have to travel the twenty-five miles into town to collect their pensions and child allowances, and post their parcels, et cetera. In these modern, cost-conscious times, Little Gidding's sub-post office was a luxury the Post Office could no longer afford. Or would no longer continue to afford once Miss Holliday went.

After that little bombshell, there was no more talk of petitions; and when Big John Little, the village inebriate, stumbled about in the flower-beds beneath Miss Holliday's bedroom window late one night shaking his huge fist and bawling out to her that she was a mouldy old witch he wished were dead and that the day she died there would be dancing in the streets, he was anxiously bundled away from the scene by some of the other villagers in case Someone Up There heard and took pity and the wish became a deed. Travelling back and forth to Gidding, the nearest town to the village, on post-office business didn't bear thinking about!

CHAPTER 2

Two more senior citizens, a Mrs. Pearson and her friend, Daphne Cross—like Miss Sayer, both clutching their pension books—came into the store. They moved up to the post-office counter and formed a queue behind Miss Sayer, waited patiently for a few moments, then glanced questioningly at one another and peeked round Miss Sayer at the postmistress' back. Nobody said anything. After a few more moments of absolute quiet, the two women standing behind Miss Sayer began to whisper between themselves. Miss Sayer stared resolutely to the front and refused to be drawn into their conversation, which grew steadily louder and was intended for her ears. But the hoped-for inquiries concerning the council-organised holiday to Swansea which the two women proposed to take the following week never materialised. Miss Sayer steadfastly refused even to acknowledge the other women's presence. Her cheeks and the back of her neck where it showed between the collar of her mauve linen suit and the tight, springy white curls which had escaped the confines of her pleated, mauve-and-white cloche hat, grew pinker.

A swarthy-looking man of about fifty in tight faded jeans and a chest-hugging, see-through white Indian cotton shirt joined the queue. The man, whose name was Curry, made model aeroplanes and helicopters and ran a small mail-order business supplying model aircraft kits and spares. He came into the post office most days at this time to dispatch the previous day's mail. (He ran the business single-handedly and was always at least one day behind with his orders.) He was formerly a schoolteacher, his last teaching post being with a

North Yorkshire junior school from which he had been requested to resign following a determined campaign against him organised by the parents who strongly objected to his progressive ideas. A chunky gold identity bracelet dangled over the bundle of mail he was carrying in his right hand, and nestling in the matted, fuzzy dark hair covering his broad chest was a heavy gold medallion on a thick gold chain. His shirt, which was neatly tucked in at the waist of his jeans, was unbuttoned and disappeared in a sharp V behind his belt-buckle.

The two pensioners standing ahead of him in the post-office queue had stopped talking and turned as he had entered the store, staring at him openly. They knew Rafe Curry by sight, but were so absorbed with their own private thoughts about his overall casual appearance that neither returned his polite greeting. Then, giving one another a furtive sidelong look, they waited expectantly for Miss Sayer to turn round and say something. Surprisingly, Miss Sayer's personal sentiments about hairy-chested males who wore loud gold jewellery and didn't button up their shirts in the presence of ladies were not known. But she was sure not to let the moment pass without making some comment—Miss Sayer was notorious for her outspoken views—and, if she were in anything like her usual form, give them something to talk about over lunch at the Day Centre.

However, Mr. Curry, who hadn't been living in the village for very long—less than six months—was spared for another day. Miss Sayer, almost as if she feared that any deviation in her concentration on Miss Holliday's back would increase the period of waiting, did not look round.

Clutched in Mr. Curry's left hand was a long, thin brown-paper parcel which contained the blade of a model helicopter which he had repaired for a Saudi princeling. The young prince was a good customer of his, and Mr. Curry had made a special effort with the repair work and had hoped to catch the midday air parcel post, the last in the village for today, this being half-day closing. He cast a vaguely concerned eye over the situation, noted the three pension books ahead of him, and calculated what this probably meant in terms of a further delay. Then he said, loudly but cheerfully, "Shop!"

Because it was Rafe Curry (Miss Holliday recognised his voice), and because she feared that his shirt-buttons would be undone all the way down to his waist again, her face reddened. Mr. Curry was unique amongst her customers, the exception which proved the rule. He was the only person she looked straight in the eye as opposed to a point which hovered somewhere between a customer's waist and right shoulder. This practice was adopted after her first encounter with his hairy chest, which had really rattled her, given her a peculiar tingling sensation in her groin which had confused and upset her for days because she had never experienced anything like it before—and never wanted to again. For his part, Mr. Curry was one of the few who could honestly claim to be more familiar with the village postmistress' face than the crown of her head.

Woodenly, and without looking round, Miss Holliday repeated what she had told Miss Sayer several minutes earlier, that she was on her own. He would have to be patient.

Mr. Curry, who was occasionally sufficiently provoked by Miss Holliday to get out his car and drive into Gidding with his mail, said dryly, "Well, every cloud has its silver lining, I suppose. It could be worse: we could all be putting down roots here for nothing more than one first-class stamp apiece."

The third woman in the queue, Mrs. Pearson, looked round at him and said, not too brightly, "There's a dispenser out in front of the store if a stamp's all you want."

"Yes, love," he said patiently. "I know. I heard about the petition lobbying your M.P. to press the Post Office to provide you with one . . . counter service being what it is round here."

Mrs. Pearson glanced anxiously at Miss Holliday's back, but there was no reaction from her. At any other time, Mrs. Pearson would have enjoyed Mr. Curry's resigned sarcasm at their postmistress' expense. But today Mrs. Pearson had a query for Miss Holliday—one she had put off making for days—concerning her invalid sister's pension book; and query Miss Holliday about something, anything, and she became rather like the magistrate who sits all day passing fines for minor traffic offences. Break the magistrate's rhythm by daring to plead "not guilty," or to waste his time further by appearing in his court with tiresome excuses, and it was said that such a magistrate would come down on an offender like a ton of bricks, and a routine £25 fine could suddenly sky-rocket to £50 or even £100. So it was with Miss Holliday if you dared to break the rhythm of her day's work. And particularly with tiresome queries about incorrectly addressed pension books. . . .

Someone came into the store, and a moment later, Tilly emerged from the stock-room carrying a cardboard carton of South African canned sliced peaches. The store manageress smiled and exchanged Good-mornings with the woman who was waiting to be served.

"Another lovely day," said Tilly. "Looks like we're actually going to get that long, hot summer Stan North's been promising us. I was looking at the hedgerows only this morning as I was on my way to work and . . ."

Tilly went on chatting happily about her observations of the countryside, which, it seemed, coincided in every particular with the comments Stan North had made on television last night.

Miss Sayer shot Tilly a withering look. Silly cat, she thought irritably. If one more person said anything about the weather, she'd go mad! And as for Stan North and that ridiculous hat he wore with all the twigs sticking out of it . . . Everyone knew he was a Peeping Tom. Spying, that was what he was really doing: lurking about in the hedgerows watching the couples who pulled up in their cars by the roadside for a picnic and then got carried away with themselves in the fields. He'd been queer in the head ever since that young slut of a wife of his had picked up their baby daughters and cleared off with the insurance man. . . .

Miss Sayer's eyes narrowed as she gazed at the woman to whom Tilly was speaking. Mrs. High-and-Mighty Charles. Tilly fawning all over her. . . . It made Miss Sayer sick to listen to her. Edwina Charles was nothing but a common seaside fortune-teller, yet anybody would think she was landed gentry. They were all the same. Even David, *her own flesh and blood*, Miss Sayer snorted to herself, as good as tugged his forelock at the mention of her name.

"Humph," said the old lady disgustedly.

"Did you say something, Miss Sayer?" Mrs. Pearson inquired anxiously.

Miss Sayer looked at her sourly, didn't reply.

Unfortunately, Mrs. Pearson's nervous disposition was such that a rebuff, particularly one from Miss Sayer, whose wrath she feared even more than that of the village postmistress, made her all the more anxious, and garrulous with it.

"Have you got your ticket for lunch, Miss Sayer?" she asked with all the sycophantic solicitude of a true coward. There was a long drawn-out pause, an embarrassing silence. Then, flustered but undeterred, Mrs. Pearson looked at her companion and said, "We went down first thing this morning and got ours, didn't we, Daphne?"

Daphne Cross took one look at the expression on Miss Sayer's face and wisely kept out of it.

"Not much point, is there?" snapped Miss Sayer. "Not today."

The other two women knew what she meant. The council-run Day Centre, which five days a week provided a hot lunch for senior citizens at a fraction of its real cost, had undergone radical changes in the past twelve months since Government-imposed cut-backs in council spending. For some old people it was the increase in charges (still modest) which they objected to; while others, notably Margaret Sayer, were disgruntled about the council's insistence that every Wednesday the Day Centre must play host at lunch to the handicapped patients from several of the council's residential homes, giving them a change of scene, a day out. Miss Sayer bitterly resented having to wait on these (for her part) unwelcome guests, all of whom were in wheelchairs, some quite severely physically handicapped.

"They're like that silly cat Tilly Cockburn's husband," she fumed to her nephew, David, the last time he visited her. "They like being waited on hand and foot." (Tilly's husband, who had contracted multiple sclerosis five years ago, had lately become confined to a wheelchair: however, Miss Sayer claimed he had always been "tired," bone idle like all the Cockburns, even as a small boy, and needed pushing around in a chair of one sort of another.)

Miss Sayer looked to the front. Miss Holliday had turned and was staring past her queue of customers at the woman Tilly was serving.

Hullo, somebody's in for a wigging! thought Miss Sayer, wrongly assuming from the intent expression on the postmistress' face that it was something Tilly had either said or was doing which had caught her attention.

The old lady looked round quickly again to see what Tilly was up to, but Tilly was no longer there. Her customer, Edwina Charles the clairvoyante, who lived on the outskirts of the village, was standing alone at the counter, apparently waiting for Tilly to fetch something from the stock-room.

Miss Holliday spoke and Miss Sayer looked back at her. The postmistress was staring fixedly at the clear space beneath the post-office window, waiting for Miss Sayer to push her pension book through to her.

Miss Holliday worked her way unhurriedly and efficiently through the queue, glancing up every so often to see what was going on in the store. Tilly had filled Mrs. Charles's order and was now deep in conversation with her. Miss Holliday strained her ears, but it was impossible to hear what they were talking about over Mrs. Pearson's persistent jabbering. Impatiently, Miss Holliday cut in on Mrs. Pearson, coldly informing her that either Mrs. Pearson or her sister would have to write off about the mistake in the pension book, which would have to be returned whence it came for correction. Yes, Miss Holliday would give her the address to write to; and no, Miss Holliday would *not* write the letter for her. They must do that for themselves.

Miss Holliday was weighing the model helicopter blade on the parcel post scales when Mrs. Charles moved through the store to the post office and stood behind Mr. Curry. Miss Holliday, who had turned side on to her customers while she checked the weight of Mr. Curry's parcel, watched the clairvoyante out of the corner of an eye.

Mr. Curry completed his business, turned and greeted Mrs. Charles, who was a near neighbour, and then he went out. The clairvoyante moved up to the window. Miss Holliday was making a note of the destination of Mr. Curry's air parcel in a little book she took out of a drawer in the counter.

Mrs. Charles waited patiently for the postmistress to attend to her. Wisely, the clairvoyante allowed herself plenty of time when she wanted to do any business at the village post office. Miss Holliday kept everybody waiting—Mrs. Charles was not so vain as to imagine that Miss Holliday was in any way reserving this special treatment for her—but for the past few weeks, the postmistress had definitely been rather more pointed about it, quite deliberately turning away from the window as the clairvoyante would move up to be served and pretending to be busy with something on the back counter. Mrs. Charles assumed that this was the postmistress' way of registering her annoyance over the increasing amount of foreign airmail the clairvoyante had been sending out since agreeing temporarily to handle the mail received by a celebrated high society astrologist while the latter recovered her health after a serious illness. All this weighing of mail, in some instances to countries Miss Holliday was only vaguely aware existed, seriously disrupted her flow. It really irritated her to have to keep referring to the overseas' postal rates compendium for the correct postage on foreign mail. But not today. The clairvoyante's eyes widened fractionally in surprise as the postmistress attended to her immediately after she had completed her notation about Mr. Curry's parcel and returned the air parcel book to the drawer.

Mumbling something to the effect that if they were quick, they might catch the midday post, Miss Holliday gathered up the clairvoyante's mail and began to weigh the individual letters, neatly marking in the top right-hand corner of each the cost of postage according to destination. As a rule, Miss Holliday rapidly called out the postage after she had weighed each piece of mail and consulted the appropriate postal rates compendium, and it was up to the clairvoyante to sort out afterwards what went where.

More than just a little bemused by this totally uncharacteristic behaviour on Miss Holliday's part, Mrs. Charles stamped her mail, thanked the postmistress and turned away from the counter. Miss Holliday's eyes followed her all the way to the door, where the clairvoyante abruptly paused and looked back over her shoulder.

The postmistress' face flooded with colour, and she quickly lowered her gaze and moved from the window, busying herself with the bulging sack of mail under the back counter.

The clairvoyante continued to look back into the post-office stores. For a split second, the warmth went out of the day and the shadows lengthened. The clairvoyante's eyes darkened. She would see Miss Holliday again that day. Miss Holliday had something on her mind, something which was becoming an obsession with her, a matter of life and death. . . .

Thoughtfully, Mrs. Charles stepped out into the glaring midday sunshine and posted her mail in the red pillar box at the front of the post-office stores, then started back through the drowsy village towards her home. The main thoroughfare was deserted save for herself and Margaret Sayer, who was standing at the roadside near the tiny foot-bridge over the duck pond. The old lady was muttering crossly to herself as she searched through the contents of her handbag for her lunch ticket, which she had bought soon after ten that morning. Miss Sayer hadn't yet missed a Wednesday at the Day Centre, though to hear her talk one could not be blamed for thinking that she never went anywhere near the place on this particular day of the week.

Immediately to Miss Sayer's left, a large black-and-white road sign warned drivers of motor vehicles, Slow Ducks Crossing. Crammed at an oblique angle between Slow and Ducks was the word "old," which had been spray-painted on the white background in a wavering hand. A car driver, observing the sign and smiling to himself, dutifully pulled up as Miss Sayer, having found the missing ticket, stepped down from the kerb on to the roadway and crossed.

CHAPTER 3

Some people said the village had not changed in centuries, but as little as thirty years ago it had been a very different place. In those days the post office and local telephone exchange had operated out of the front room of Agatha Dunphie's cottage, and one conducted one's business through the window which had been suitably altered for the purpose. There were only three telephones in the village then, and no village store. A van called regularly at the village every Tuesday with groceries for the villagers who left their orders with Miss Dunphie before 9:30 A.M. that same day. Miss Dunphie then telephoned the orders through to the grocer in Gidding who provided the once-weekly delivery service.

This arrangement, which continued for many years without interruption, ceased when the Gidding grocer sold out to one of the large supermarket chains. They thought it rather quaint of him to provide this service, but then so was the horse and buggy, and like the horse and buggy, Little Gidding would simply have to move with the times. The villagers would have to visit the supermarket personally like everyone else. There could be no preferential treatment. They were sorry that Little Gidding had (at that time) such a high percentage of aged and infirm residents, none of whom had their own private transport, but business was business.

Miss Dunphie had other ideas. She was so outraged and incensed by the callously indifferent tone of the letters she received from the supermarket's various spokespeople refuting her claim that Little Gidding and several other outlying villages were special cases and refusing her request that some provision be made for them, that she applied for, and was

granted, planning permission to build an extension on to Rose
Cottage to house the sub-post office and a grocery store.

It was to be Miss Dunphie's undoing. The extra work involved steadily undermined her health to the point where she
could no longer carry on alone. Her hands became crippled
with arthritis from all the heavy lifting and carrying entailed
in the running of a grocery business; and then, after a succes-
sion of minor illnesses, diabetes mellitus was diagnosed. Her
doctor, when he confirmed the diagnosis, gave her very little
choice. She could sell up, retire—and he strongly advised that
it would be in her best interests if she were to make arrangements to do so immediately—or she would have to engage full-
time permanent staff, find someone to manage the grocery
store for her, and employ a counter assistant in the post office.
Without a second's hesitation, Miss Dunphie chose the second
of these alternatives.

The vacancy in the store was quickly filled. But finding
someone good at figure work and prepared to undergo the necessary training for the position in the post office was quite a
different matter.

A slow-moving procession of bored housewives filled the
post while Miss Dunphie assessed their potential, but ultimately they all found the job even more boring than house-
work and were only too glad to return to the latter when Miss
Dunphie tactfully suggested that this would probably be best
all round.

The next applicant for the post was a seventeen-year-old
youth whose mother assured Miss Dunphie that he was bril-
liant at maths, top of his class. His simple arithmetic, however,
drove Miss Dunphie to the point of near despair, with the result that this young man's post-office career progressed no further than a preliminary interview.

In desperation, Miss Dunphie cast her net wider to take in
neighbouring villages and, finally, Gidding, where she adver-
tised the position, without success, in the local newspaper all
through the month of April and then, as a last resort, asked a
friend in the town, who ran a newsagency, to put a situations

vacant card in his shop window. That card eventually produced Miss Holliday.

For the first three months, the new counter assistant was seen in the post office only. Then one day it was observed that Miss Holliday no longer travelled to the village from Gidding every morning in the red mail van with the postman. (There was no regular bus service in those days.) She was now living in the village at Rose Cottage with Miss Dunphie. There was considerable speculation about where all this was going to lead, particularly amongst those who were not too enthralled with the plump, pale-faced, withdrawn new counter assistant who did her job efficiently enough but never smiled and rarely, if ever, looked up. It was also rightly assumed by those same people that Arthur Dunphie's nose would be badly put out of joint by this unexpected turn of events. But even so, no one guessed or even suspected that it would result in the young man's disinheritance by the aunt who had raised him and with whom he had remained on the best of terms right up until her death, despite her disapproval of his means of making a living for himself. In deference to his aunt's wishes, he usually described himself as an accountant, but in reality, Arthur Dunphie had made a moderately successful career out of a compulsion. He was a professional gambler.

Arthur had threatened to take legal action when Miss Dunphie's executors had acquainted him with the contents of her will, but had been advised against it by his solicitors. He could not be said to be in desperate financial need; nor could he prove his claim that Miss Holliday had unduly influenced his aunt to change her will. Even Arthur had to admit that this was really little more than wishful thinking. No one had observed his aunt and Miss Holliday together closer than he had, and Miss Holliday was never anything but perfectly polite and respectful to his aunt, subservient almost. And the fact that Miss Holliday was probably incapable of showing Miss Dunphie's caring concern and affection for people was hardly a basis for the kind of litigation Arthur had in mind.

The news that Miss Dunphie's only surviving relative had

been cut off without a penny had left the villagers stunned for days. They hadn't been able to understand it. Miss Dunphie had been such a good, kind, *sensible* woman.

As the years went by and the villagers got to know their new postmistress a little better, they too began to share Arthur Dunphie's suspicions about her. In the same quiet way that she bullied and terrorised them into submission, so had poor Miss Dunphie become terrorised and bullied into submission.

This widely held belief made the villagers feel very bitter towards Miss Holliday over her acquisition of Rose Cottage and the post-office stores. They also felt guilty, ashamed of themselves for having stood by and let it happen. It was awful to think that someone who had always shown so much selfless regard and consideration for others should have been abandoned by those very same people in her hour of need and left at the mercy of a terrible woman like Miss Holliday.

However, if they could have their time all over again, turn back the clock, as many of them so often wished in this regard, Miss Dunphie would undoubtedly have explained to them why she had cut Arthur completely out of her will. Again the villagers themselves had been the prime mover in her decision to leave Rose Cottage and the post-office stores to Miss Holliday and not to her nephew. It was her concern for the elderly, the young mothers with small children in perambulators or pushchairs, the appallingly inadequate public transport system linking Little Gidding with neighbouring villages and towns, and the strong rumour going around, even then, that the village post office was doomed, which influenced Miss Dunphie when drawing up a new will. She knew that if she left her cottage and the post-office stores to Arthur, he would instruct her executors to convert everything into hard cash as soon as practicable (and probably lose the lot on a single turn of the roulette wheel at one of the fancy clubs he frequented in London); and while the new owner of Rose Cottage would no doubt wish to continue with the grocery store, the sale might be used as an excuse to close down the sub-post office. Miss Dunphie had an off-the-record meeting with the Head Postmaster in Gidding about the matter, and while he could give her no guarantees, he expressed the personal opinion that there might possibly be second thoughts about the rumoured closure if Miss Dunphie were to leave the village store to her fully trained counter assistant. This proved to be the case. The village post office was granted a stay of execution, but only for so long as Miss Holliday remained at the helm, as was later pointed out to the villagers in response to their petition to have her removed from her post.

Miss Dunphie never once considered the possibility that Miss Holliday might one day wish to forsake everything she had in the village for a man and marriage. The old postmistress privately agreed with her nephew that Miss Holliday was a cold fish. Not once in all the years during which they had worked and lived under the same roof together had Miss Dunphie detected the tiniest spark of warmth in her young helper. But she had made an excellent assistant and in most respects, would make a first-rate postmistress. Miss Dunphie was a realist. She knew she couldn't have everything. And neither could the villagers. She could only hope that in time they would come to understand and accept her better judgment. Perhaps even pity their new young postmistress. It was a sad thing, certainly one of the saddest things Miss Dunphie could think of, not to care anything for one's fellow man and to be as hard and ungiving as Miss Holliday was. Many an hour Miss Dunphie had spent agonising over this flaw in her assistant's personality and indeed had felt something of a failure because she had been unable to penetrate the protective armour the young woman always wore. After having spent the best part of ten years in one another's company, day in and day out, Miss Dunphie was about as close to Miss Holliday as she was to the man in the moon. She knew what Miss Holliday liked for breakfast. That she loathed green vegetables and positively refused to eat Brussels sprouts, which nauseated her so badly she would retch at the mere sight of them. That it was only with the greatest reluctance that Miss Holliday would enter a church, any church (and yet her knowledge of the

Bible was often quite astonishing). That grey was her favourite colour; and that she didn't like clocks, and while putting on a brave face about it when asked to climb up on a chair and wind it, was—for some curious reason Miss Dunphie never fathomed—terrified of the antique one in the store.

There was little else that Miss Dunphie could have told any-one about her young assistant. She wasn't sure if Miss Holliday had any family. She didn't think so. Miss Holliday had never mentioned anybody, and Miss Dunphie had been anxious not to distress the young woman with this kind of probing if there were something in her past which she preferred not to discuss. It was, thought Miss Dunphie, none of her business. No one's business until Miss Holliday chose to make it otherwise.

CHAPTER 4

Margaret Sayer was enjoying a cup of tea alone in her sitting-room when Miss Holliday walked quickly down the road past her window, which struck Miss Sayer as being quite uncanny. She had only just been thinking about Miss Holliday, her actual appearance in person this far from Rose Cottage and the post-office stores all the more remarkable for the infrequency of such an occurrence. Miss Sayer could not remember ever having seen Miss Holliday out and about on this side of the village, certainly not on foot. Miss Holliday seldom ventured out other than in her car.

Miss Sayer watched her thoughtfully over the rim of her teacup. The Day Centre had been buzzing with gossip and speculation about the village postmistress at lunch, making this one of the few Wednesdays that Miss Sayer had returned home in the afternoon in a reasonably good humour and with something on her mind other than the once-weekly upset the visitors to the Day Centre inflicted upon her digestive system. Mavis Tavistock, the voluntary worker who accompanied the Day Centre's Wednesday visitors, had brought the news. She said she had it on good authority that that nice Mr. Smith, the resident superintendent of St. Anthony's Village, was courting a young woman. And not just any young woman. Miss Holliday. *Their* Miss Holliday from the village post office. They had been seen together on a number of occasions in and around Gidding and at least once out driving in the countryside in Mr. Smith's nice new car.

Miss Sayer made a peculiar little snorting noise at the back of her nose. It was all absolute nonsense, of course. Mavis Tavistock was as silly as a wheel, wouldn't know what day of

the week it was. And as soon as Miss Sayer had finished her
tea, she intended to telephone a friend who lived in one of the
small, single-storey home-units St. Anthony's had built in an
attractive village setting on a large acreage of land in South
Gidding, which had been donated to the Church for the care
and protection of elderly distressed gentlewomen, and check
out Mavis Tavistock's story. Very possibly, Mr. Smith was
courting a young lady—after all, it was almost two years now
since his wife Olive had died and he was still a comparatively
young man—but it was not Miss Holliday. Miss Sayer refused
to believe it.

"As different as chalk is to cheese," she said out loud as she
continued to watch Miss Holliday's progress down the middle
of the road. (Just asking to get run down by one of those luna-
tics who forgot they were no longer on the motorway and
came racing hell for leather past her front door on their way
into the village.) Besides, thought Miss Sayer with a dismissive
snort, Jocelyn Smith was old enough to be Miss Holliday's father. Well, *almost* old enough. . . .

Miss Sayer moved her chair further into the bay window so
she could continue watching Miss Holliday without getting a
painful crick in her neck. She couldn't think why Miss Holliday should be walking down the road in that particular direction, towards the motorway, at this hour of the day. Unless she
was going to call on that lazy Mr. Curry. Maybe there had
been some further trouble between them after she had left the
post office that morning and Miss Holliday was calling on him
about it.

No. Most unlikely, Miss Sayer decided. The mountain would
summon Mohammet to her. Especially if the bone she had to
pick with him was concerned with post-office business. And
that soppy Molly Pearson would've said something at lunch if
there had been a disagreement of some kind between Miss
Holliday and Mr. Curry after she (Miss Sayer) had left the
post office.

So Miss Holliday wasn't calling on Mr. Curry.

Maybe her car had broken down and she hoped to hitch a lift into Gidding. . . .

Even more unlikely. Miss Holliday asked favours of no one. She would walk into Gidding first. Crawl on her hands and knees.

Mrs. Charles?

The old lady's eyes narrowed.

So that was why Miss Holliday was staring so hard at Edwina Charles this morning. . . .

Miss Sayer rose and crossed quickly to the sideboard, got out the opera-glasses her grandmother had left her, and then hurried outside and stood at her front gate watching Miss Holliday through them.

The postmistress had reached the clairvoyante's bungalow. She paused momentarily, put a hand on the wrought-iron front gate, then quickly took it away as if the metal were hot and had scorched her flesh. She turned away, started back towards the village.

Miss Sayer continued to watch her through the small binoculars. She couldn't see Miss Holliday's face clearly. Miss Holliday always walked about with her head down, eyes searching the ground. But there was something about her manner, a stiffness of posture, which suggested that she might be close to panic. In fact, after looking shrinkingly back over her shoulder at the clairvoyante's bungalow, Miss Holliday noticeably quickened her pace. But then, just as Miss Sayer was about to retreat quickly inside out of sight, Miss Holliday paused, looked back over her shoulder again.

Haunted, thought Miss Sayer, her eyes riveted to the opera-glasses. That was how Miss Holliday looked. Sick to her stomach.

No sooner had the thought entered Miss Sayer's head than the postmistress rushed to the side of the road and was sick in a ditch.

Curiouser and curiouser, thought Miss Sayer.

Slowly Miss Holliday straightened up, wiped her face with her handkerchief, then her hands.

Miss Sayer watched her intently, waited. She knew instinctively that Miss Holliday would retrace her steps to the clairvoyante's bungalow. Just as soon as she had composed herself.

Meanwhile, Miss Sayer concentrated her gaze on the man who had been repairing the rear side fence of one of a pair of semi-detached farm-workers' cottages situated roughly midway between Miss Sayer's cottage and where Miss Holliday was now standing. The man, Big John Little, had stopped what he was doing and stared as Miss Holliday had passed the cottage where he was working, and then sauntered casually out to the road. Propping himself up against a tree, he got out his tobacco pouch and unhurriedly began to roll a cigarette.

Miss Sayer was furious. She had been waiting ages for Big John to come and put a new withy hurdle in her back fence where it had been breached by the local hunt last winter when the fox had taken temporary refuge in her garden. Twice now she had been awakened by cows mooing below her bedroom window. Not to mention the damage they were doing in her garden. At the rate things were going, she thought crossly as Big John lit up his cigarette, she soon wouldn't have any garden to worry about. . . .

Miss Sayer stiffened. Miss Holliday had suddenly moved.

Reluctantly—Miss Sayer was quite sure about this—Miss Holliday turned back towards the clairvoyante's bungalow.

Miss Sayer's gaze switched momentarily to Big John (who was thoughtfully scratching his broad, fat belly), then back again to Miss Holliday.

What on earth would Miss Holliday want with a fortune-teller? Miss Sayer asked herself.

She kept her eyes glued to the opera-glasses. She couldn't believe what she was thinking. . . .

There was something in what Mavis Tavistock had said at lunch after all, and Miss Holliday, like some silly, romantic schoolgirl, was looking to have her fortune told.

She must actually hope, or think, she is going to marry Mr. Smith, Miss Sayer realised with a shock.

Her? Mae Holliday, who wouldn't lift a finger to help any-

*body if she could possibly avoid it, thought she was going to
be the wife of the superintendent of St. Anthony's Village?*

Miss Sayer shook her head. Her thin lips set in a determined
line.

Over her dead body!

She was about to go indoors and make her telephone call to
her friend when something caught her eye.

Mr. Curry was standing in his living-room window, which
was at the side of his cottage, making what appeared to be a
rude, two-fingered gesture at her.

Rigid with indignation, Miss Sayer stamped inside, slamming the door behind her. Just what she'd expect of an Arab.
Mr. Curry might think he'd fooled the others, but he hadn't
fooled her. She knew an infidel when she saw one. You only
had to look at all that black hair on his chest. . . .

The opera-glasses were unceremoniously shoved back in the
sideboard.

Made model aeroplanes, did he? Miss Sayer sneered scep-
tically to herself as she wrestled with the drawer, which was
stiff and heavy and difficult to close. A likely story!

CHAPTER 5

The door opened—almost, thought Miss Holliday uneasily, as if the clairvoyante had been expecting her.

The postmistress spoke falteringly, well before the door was properly open. "I hope I haven't caught you at an inconvenient moment, Mrs. Charles." Miss Holliday forced herself to look directly at the clairvoyante, but the strain was too much and she lowered her eyes almost immediately to the coir mat on which she was standing, kept them downcast as she continued. "I know you are a very busy person, and I wouldn't wish to intrude. That's if, er . . ." Miss Holliday paused, coloured. "That is, I thought you might have one of your clients with you. I know I should have said something to you this morning while you were in the post office, but—"

Miss Holliday broke off and put the back of her right hand quickly to her pale, perspiring forehead and held it there. "I'm sorry," she said breathlessly. "It's this heat. I feel rather faint. Do you think I might come in and sit down for a moment? Just say if I'm making a nuisance of myself; I won't take offence."

The clairvoyante looked at her thoughtfully, without speaking, then stepped back and indicated that Miss Holliday should go through to the sitting-room. Mrs. Charles left her sitting on the sofa with the electric fan switched on while she went out to the kitchen and made a pot of tea.

At the sitting-room door, the clairvoyante paused briefly and looked back. Miss Holliday was unfastening the top button on her pearl-grey blouse, which had a chin-high, chokingly tight, lace-edged Victorian collar. She was a dreadful colour, a washed-out grey, like her box-pleated skirt.

The quickness with which the clairvoyante returned with

the tea reinforced Miss Holliday's belief that Mrs. Charles was expecting a visitor.

"You're quite sure I'm not intruding?" said Miss Holliday. She sat erect, looked uncomfortable, ill at ease. "You're not expecting someone, are you?"

Mrs. Charles reassured her with a slow shake of the head and a thoughtful smile. "I cancelled my appointments for the rest of the day," she said. Her smile lingered as she poured the tea. "You see, I wasn't too sure just when you would come."

The postmistress' eyes widened fractionally. "You *knew* I was going to visit you?"

The clairvoyante passed Miss Holliday her tea. Then, without looking at her: "Is it a visit, Miss Holliday?"

"I—" The postmistress gazed intently at the steaming hot liquid in the dainty bone china teacup she was holding. Then, as if there were something about it which displeased her, she put it aside.

"You wish to consult me, is that it?" The clairvoyante looked at her. "There is no need for you to feel embarrassed about it."

Miss Holliday did not say anything for a moment. Then, to the teacup which she had placed on the occasional table before her: "You don't mind?"

"It is how I make my living," the clairvoyante replied simply.

The postmistress hesitated, frowned. "I've heard it said that all your clients are rich and famous and that you charge very high fees." Miss Holliday was gazing steadily at the hem of her skirt, which had ridden up and lay across the top of her thick knees. "I know what they say about me in the village. Everyone thinks I inherited a fortune from Miss Dunphie, but that's not true." She paused, carefully pleated the hem of her skirt, then smoothed it flat across her knees again. "It was reported in the *Sketch* . . . the net value of her estate. For everyone to see. There was no cash to speak of; only the property—the cottage and the post-office stores." She looked up briefly. Then, with a small shrug: "I am not a wealthy woman, Mrs. Charles. The pittance I receive from the Post Office they defend with the argument that it's post-office business that brings potential customers into my store, I should be grateful. But these days the store barely breaks even. So many people have cars now. And with that new hypermarket opening up in Gidding a few years ago . . . well, most of the villagers go there now and buy in bulk. They only come to me in an emergency, if they run short of something—"

Mrs. Charles interrupted her.

"I think we should first of all establish whether or not I can be of service to you. Then we will discuss the other matter." The clairvoyante spoke softly, smiled kindly, but there was a certain wariness in her eyes. She looked at Miss Holliday for a moment longer, then she nodded her head and said, "Now drink up your tea."

"You're very kind," Miss Holliday mumbled, even more embarrassed, reluctantly taking up her cup and saucer again. "I—I'm not sure that I deserve it."

"Everyone deserves a little kindness, Miss Holliday," the clairvoyante replied.

Miss Holliday suddenly leaned forward and placed her tea, untouched, on the tray, pushed the tray away from her. "I could be a little kinder to people, is that what you're saying?"

"You are what you are, Miss Holliday," said the clairvoyante.

The postmistress looked up, then looked quickly away. "But that's just it," she said, so quietly that the clairvoyante could barely hear her. "I'm not. I don't know who I am or what I am. All I know is what and who other people *think* I am."

"I don't think I understand what you mean," said the clairvoyante.

Miss Holliday stretched the hem of her skirt taut across her knees. "I'm a fake, a fraud, Mrs. Charles," she said, again very quietly. "I'm one great big sixteen-year-long lie. I'm nobody. That's who I am. Only that's not really true, is it?" Her voice had steadily risen and become edgy, a little shrill. "Everybody's somebody, somebody from somewhere. That's what I want you to help me to remember. I want you to look in the crystal ball or the cards—the Tarot—and tell me who I really am." She started to laugh, a nervous, choking sound which hung uncomfortably on the air. "Shall I tell you something funny? Some people celebrate birthdays. Me? The only thing I've got to celebrate is the anniversary of my name. The May Spring Bank Holiday—next Monday week is my big day for celebration. The May Bank Holiday and Miss Mae Holliday." She looked up at Mrs. Charles and her eyes were wide, staring. "You don't see the connection?"

"Are you telling me that Holliday isn't your real name?"

Miss Holliday continued to stare at her for a moment longer, then abruptly she dropped her gaze.

"I made it up," she said shortly. "Changed the spelling: substituted an *e* for the *y* in "May" and put two *l*'s in "holiday." You can't go very far without a name, you know," she said sullenly. "And you'd be surprised just how many times you're asked to give a name when you don't have one."

"I'm still not sure I know what your real problem is," the clairvoyante confessed after a small silence. "If you're saying you're illegitimate and you wish to trace your real parents—"

"No," said Miss Holliday sharply. She shook her head. "I don't want to know who they are; I don't care who they are; I'm not even all that bothered if I am illegitimate. I only want to know, to be able to remember, who *I* am. I *must* know who I am before I—" She didn't finish.

"Before what?" the clairvoyante asked quietly.

The other woman said woodenly, "I'd rather not say, if you don't mind. It's one of those things . . ." She shrugged. "If I'm unable to find out who I really am, it might never happen, so it's best kept right out of things. And in any event, it has no bearing whatsoever on the matter."

Mrs. Charles sat back in her chair with her tea and sipped it thoughtfully. She studied the postmistress for several moments before speaking again. Then, softly: "Have you been to a private detective?"

"I thought about it once," Miss Holliday confessed. "I even made an appointment with one in Gidding, but right at the last minute I changed my mind about seeing him and spent the afternoon in a cinema instead."

"Why?"

Miss Holliday hesitated, frowned. "I'm not really sure. I guess I was afraid of what he might discover about me."

"And you're not afraid now?"

Miss Holliday, eyes downcast, nodded. "Yes, I'm just as afraid, but I know you . . ." She looked up. Then, with flickering eyelids: "They say in the village that you . . ." She paused, steadied her gaze, then looked down at her lap. "It's common knowledge that you have something of a shady past, and I thought that if there turned out to be something, well, shady, in my past, you wouldn't make trouble for me. You'd understand and keep it to yourself. You don't tittle-tattle like the rest of them do."

"I see," said the clairvoyante slowly, nodding her head.

"You're offended," said the postmistress dully, "and I can't say I blame you. Tact was never one of my strong points. Leopards can't change their spots, you know. I've always said what I think. I can't bear hypocrisy, even if in speaking the truth, saying what I think, I seem shallow to some people."

There was a long silence.

"Well?" Miss Holliday demanded at length. She looked at Mrs. Charles anxiously. "Will you help me?"

The clairvoyante did not answer immediately. Unhurriedly, she rose from her chair and placed her cup and saucer on the tray with Miss Holliday's. Then, resuming her seat, and after a further pause, she said, "If I've understood your problem correctly and you are an amnesiac, you should really consult a doctor—"

"And what? Have my business all over the village in five minutes flat? Have people say I'm off my head?" Miss Holliday's chin shot up defiantly. "It's my memory I've lost, not my senses!"

"You could see someone outside the village. There are many fine doctors you could consult in Gidding who would, I'm sure, respect your confidence."

Miss Holliday averted her gaze and said dryly, "Psychiatrists, you mean, don't you?"

Mrs. Charles did not reply.

Miss Holliday drew a deep breath. "I'm not mad, Mrs. Charles. And if it weren't for the fact that for reasons, as I've already said, I'd rather not go into right now, I feel I ought to know who I really am, I wouldn't be sitting here today asking for your help." She paused. Then, calmly: "Please understand. Being Mae Holliday suits me just fine. I like being her; I've always liked being her. I only wish I could go on being her. But unfortunately, I can't. Mae Holliday doesn't exist. Not on paper, where it really matters most."

Mrs. Charles looked at her. "You're quite sure about that?"

Miss Holliday glanced up. "Yes, quite sure. I told you, I made it up. The name . . . when I couldn't remember my real one. Sixteen years ago come the Spring Bank Holiday at the end of this month, I went to the Town Hall in Gidding to see if they had any lists of accommodation available, and the girl I spoke to there said yes, but I'd have to wait a minute, as the person who looked after that department was busy on the telephone. Then she asked me my name, and I suddenly realised I didn't know what it was, I couldn't remember it. "May holiday" was the first thought that came into my head, because of the Spring Bank Holiday—I'd watched a pageant in the town earlier that day with a May Queen on a float—so I gave the desk clerk that. I remember being very nervous and embarrassed about it. I could've kicked myself for not using Brown or Jones—some common name. I was sure she'd guess that the name I'd given her was false. But all she said was, 'Take a seat, Miss Holliday. Mr. X (I can't remember his name) won't keep you waiting very long.' And I've been Miss Holliday ever since."

"You never considered changing the name for something else?"

Miss Holliday shook her head. "I couldn't. Events overtook me. The man at the Town Hall gave me the address of a woman in Gidding who ran a kind of hostel for single homeless girls and told me to tell her he'd sent me round. I didn't dare to use a different name after that. I was afraid he'd get in touch with her later on about me, or she with him after I'd been round there fixing up somewhere to stay."

"But you did consider finding some name other than Mae Holliday?"

The postmistress hesitated. She wasn't sure, but she had a feeling that the clairvoyante didn't trust her, thought she was lying. "No, not really," Miss Holliday said slowly. "It was more a matter of my suddenly foreseeing the difficulties I would encounter should I suddenly decide to change my name to something else."

Mrs. Charles made a pyramid of her hands and rested her chin on it.

"You'll help me?" Miss Holliday asked with a frown. The steady gaze the clairvoyante had fixed on her was disconcerting, made her feel uneasy. It was as though she were a pane of glass and Mrs. Charles was looking straight through her.

"What's wrong?" asked Miss Holliday. "Why are you staring at me like that? You think I'm lying, don't you?"

Mrs. Charles lowered her hands and said, "Forgive me, I was deep in thought. I didn't mean to stare." She smiled, looked momentarily out of the leaded window at the clear blue sky beyond. "You are an intelligent woman, Miss Holliday. I'm quite sure you don't need me to tell you that some traumatic event preceded your visit to Gidding Town Hall sixteen years ago, where you claim you suddenly found yourself with no recollection of your real name and your past."

"Like an accident of some kind," said Miss Holliday quickly. "A bump on the head. I have a deep wound, a scar, on the back of my head near my right ear . . . about an inch below the hair-line."

She got up and went over to Mrs. Charles, turned her head, then drew her short, mid-brown hair aside. "See," she said eagerly.

Mrs. Charles looked. The pale flesh was perfectly smooth,

flawless. There was no evidence of a wound, any kind of wound, small or large, anywhere on the back of Miss Holliday's head or neck.

Miss Holliday returned to the sofa and sat down again. "I kept getting these terrible earaches, and when I went to the doctor about them, he examined the back of my head and found the scar. I didn't even know it was there. He said I should have an X-ray. He seemed to think that a splintered bone, or something of the sort, was pressing on a nerve—like sciatica—and causing the earaches. But I never did anything about it. About going to the hospital for a thorough check-up, that is. Oddly enough, the earaches suddenly cleared up. I never had another one. Not after he, the doctor, had told me what was probably causing them. I mean, who'd want meningitis? That was all I was concerned about; and once he'd cleared me there and said my ears were fine, it wasn't an infection causing the pain, I stopped worrying about getting earaches. Occasionally, though, when I'm feeling tired, or I'm a bit run down, I get the odd twinge or two in the middle of the scar, but otherwise it gives me no trouble at all."

"You have no recollection of how you came to hurt your head?"

"None whatsoever."

"How long after your visit to the Town Hall did the earaches start?"

"I had one that day. Only a mild attack. The really bad ones started a few weeks later, about the time I saw Miss Dunphie's card in a newsagent's window. She was looking for a counter assistant."

Mrs. Charles nodded. "How did you manage for money up until your seeking employment with Miss Dunphie?"

Miss Holliday considered the question. Then, with a tiny frown: "I found over a hundred pounds in my purse . . . this was when I went to the Town Hall. One hundred and thirty-five pounds and a few odd shillings and pence, to be a little more precise. Though by the time I went for my interview with Miss Dunphie, I was getting desperately short of cash and becoming rather worried about the situation."

"Where did you get the money? Do you know?"

Miss Holliday shook her head. "No, I've no idea." She hesitated. Then, reflectively: "That—the money and the shoulder-bag I found it in, of course—was all I had on me. Other than for the clothes I was standing up in. I had to go out and buy a cheap suitcase from Woolworth's and some other things to put in it so it wouldn't look strange to my new landlady. She would've thought it very odd if I'd moved in with only one small, zippered spotted-dog to my name."

Mrs. Charles gave her a questioning look.

"The shoulder-bag: it was cut in the shape of a dog," Miss Holliday explained. "A white one with brown spots. You pulled his tail to unzip the bag . . . something like a pyjama case, only this had a long, thin black plastic strap for wearing on the shoulder." She paused. Then, pensively: "I think I might've had it a long time. It was very shabby. Quite grubby, in fact."

"And apart from the money you say you found in it, the bag was empty?"

Miss Holliday nodded slowly, kept her eyes down.

"The money, though, was in another small purse you kept in the shoulder-bag?" said the clairvoyante.

Miss Holliday hesitated, seemed confused. "No. . . . I'm sorry if I called it a purse before. I meant the shoulder-bag. The money was loose inside it." She looked up, spoke earnestly. "There was nothing else in it, honestly." She dropped her gaze to her knees again, frowned. "Only the money, like I said. And I honestly don't know, remember, where the money came from. Or the shoulder-bag. I don't remember anything. Except . . ." She paused, nervously fingered the hem of her skirt. "Except sometimes, when I've been working hard and I'm feeling very tired and I look in a mirror. Only it's not me I see, it's someone else. Only fleetingly. And I suddenly seem very close to remembering something, who this other person is that I see instead of myself. Sometimes I think it might've been my sister, but I'm never sure; I can't remember if I had a sister. But I think I might've . . ." She was quiet for a moment. Then, glancing quickly up: "Will you look back into the past for me? Can you do that? I don't want to know what the future holds for me. I know I can cope with that, whatever it may be, good or bad."

"Then take my advice and leave the past where it is. By deliberately bringing it forward into the present, you will inevitably influence the future."

"For the worse, you mean?" Miss Holliday thought for a moment, nodded. "Yes, I think I know that this is how it'll probably be for me. But I have made up my mind." Her head tilted a little to one side as she absently straightened the pleats of her skirt. "I feel quite calm about it now; it's not upsetting me any more." She was about to continue, but something made her pause and think. Then, after a very long moment: "I was trying to remember who it was who used to say to me, 'Needs must when the devil drives,' but it's gone, I've forgotten."

She looked up and was visibly distressed, nothing like her usual controlled self. "Tell me who I am, who I was, and why, what happened to me that I can't remember. *Why* can't I remember?"

"Because you don't really want to remember," the clairvoyante replied. "The time is not yet right for you to remember. You must be patient, give yourself more time."

"But I simply *must* remember. And it has to be now. Otherwise, it'll be too late. Please help me. I know that I, of all people, don't really deserve to be helped by anyone—and I'd be lying if I said I'll try and mend my ways, because I know I can't, it's not in my nature—but I don't think you fully realise how much this means to me and how much it's costing me in lost pride and self-esteem to come here like this to you and beg. It has taken every ounce of courage I possess. If you turn me away, I don't know what I'll do, where I'll turn next. But I am determined about this. I mean to find out who I am, whatever the consequences, and no matter what it costs."

"Very well," said the clairvoyante. "I will read the Tarot cards for you."

"Only the past," said Miss Holliday quickly. "I don't want you to tell me anything about the future. Promise me you won't—" She looked at Mrs. Charles apprehensively and her voice took on an excited urgency. "Say you promise."

"I promise," said the clairvoyante.

"I want you to know that I appreciate all that you've said, the warning you've given me," Miss Holliday said nervously as the clairvoyante rose and crossed to an antique rosewood writing-bureau in the corner of the room. "I realise I'm probably influencing the future by looking back into the past. But I don't really see that it makes much difference. My future would be equally influenced by my not looking back, I feel, for the worse. And as I'm quite certain about this—that things, life, will be all the worse for me if I don't look back—I consider it a risk worth taking. Who's to say—?" She shrugged. "Looking back needn't necessarily spell doom and gloom for me. It might prove to be the best thing I ever did."

The clairvoyante did not reply. She remained standing at the writing-bureau with her back to Miss Holliday almost as if she might have been trying to remember what she had wanted from it. Then she turned. Miss Holliday gazed mesmerically at the deck of Tarot cards in the clairvoyante's right hand, watched her place them on a small round inlaid wine-table which she then brought forward and placed between them.

"What happens now?" Miss Holliday asked apprehensively.

Without answering, the clairvoyante separated the twenty-two symbolic picture cards of the Major Arcana from the deck. Then, placing them squarely in front of Miss Holliday, she said, "Clasp the cards in both hands with your wrists resting on the edge of the table."

Miss Holliday picked up the cards, held on to them tightly as directed. She looked unhesitatingly, trustingly, across the table into Mrs. Charles's eyes, and the clairvoyante watched the years roll away from her. Gone was the unfeeling bully, the dumpy, autocratic spinster who, by virtue of the powers vested in her by the Post Office, inevitably touched the lives of nearly everyone in the village. She was a child again, young, bright-eyed and eager, unsoured by life.

"Tell me again about Mae Holliday," the clairvoyante said quietly, and lightly placed her hand on Miss Holliday's.

The tension the clairvoyante could feel in the hand beneath hers slowly disappeared as the postmistress obediently retold her story. But it would not make what she said about herself any the more truthful. Merely add a little more sincerity to the lies.

CHAPTER 6

Thankfully, Vera Markham put down her shopping bags and fanned her red face with the leaflet a scruffy-looking youth had pressed upon her outside Marks & Spencer's. She looked into the faces of the equally hot shoppers in the long, ragged queue ahead of her and came to the conclusion that she must be mad. It was much too hot to be rushing around town shopping all morning and then, instead of going quietly home to a nice cup of tea and a rest on the loafer in the garden, queuing in the blazing sun for a bus to St. Anthony's Wall on market-day.

In the eleventh century, the people of Gidding had erected a high stone wall around their town and right on its front doorstep—indeed, part of the arched gateway to the town was incorporated in it—built their church, which was dedicated, in the thirteenth century, to St. Anthony of Padua, patron saint of lovers, marriage and women in confinement. Today all that remained of the town wall was the arch over the gateway and the few yards of crumbling stonework which bore the official plaque marking the spot as being of some historical interest.

The church, Anglican since the Reformation and frequently and not improperly referred to as Gidding Cathedral since it had a bishop's throne on the south side of the choir, had survived, though restoration work was constantly in progress, particularly on the magnificent stained-glass windows which were becoming alarmingly corroded by twentieth-century air pollution. The restoration of St. Anthony's was originally instigated and paid for by a wealthy seventeenth-century nobleman named Bourne, who had also built the Lady Chapel in expiation, it was said, of some terrible sin one of his sons had committed.

It was to the Bournes' Lady Chapel that Vera Markham was making her pilgrimage. She had been praying to Our Lady all week, but only from the cosy comfort of her bed late at night when the house was dark and still and the television was finally switched off for the evening and there was nothing better to do. And that wasn't good enough, she had told herself last night when she had learnt of the temporary court adjournment of her son's case after a key witness had been taken suddenly ill halfway through the trial. If she wanted Our Lady to hear her prayer and answer it, she must make some personal sacrifice, suffer a little hardship and inconvenience. And this, she thought, as she collected up her heavy shopping bags and surged forward with everyone else in the queue, then struggled unaided aboard the crowded green bus which had drawn into the kerb, was exactly what she was doing—making a martyr of herself.

As an Anglican, Vera Markham would not normally have considered praying to Our Lady. But this was something special, something she felt only another mother would understand; and this was how she intended to speak to Our Lady today in Her Chapel—as one distraught mother to another. A final entreaty.

It was half past midday when Vera Markham finally limped with swollen ankles and a blistered right heel across St. Anthony's Square to the church. The cobbled, medieval, completely shadeless square was busy. Office-workers in their lunch break used it as a shortcut to the market which was held every Thursday in Monks Lane off the square. Vera Markham glanced to her left at the canvas-covered stalls and the crowds of people milling about the lane, thought how glad she was not to be amongst that little lot in all this sticky heat, then painfully climbed the wide stone steps to the church and crossed the cool flagged porch. She felt self-conscious about taking her shopping inside with her and would have preferred to leave it on the porch, but she didn't dare. Those with no conscience about stealing sacred artefacts from the church in broad daylight wouldn't think twice about helping themselves to anything left unattended in the porch. With pilfering from churches on the increase, Vera Markham had even been a little concerned that her trip might be in vain, St. Anthony's would be closed to the public. So many places of worship were these days. Some people, thought Vera Markham, as she passed silently in front of the font at the back of the church, would steal the pew from behind you while you knelt to pray.

Her thick, crêpe-soled sandals made no sound. The church, with its high, vaulted ceiling and imposing wooden beams, was deathly quiet. But she was not alone. A small groan of dismay escaped her lips. A woman—Vera Markham just glimpsed a final swish of a woman's grey box-pleated skirt—had gone into the tiny Lady Chapel and was now drawing the plush purple velvet curtain which screened it off from the church proper and ensured that she would not be disturbed while at her devotions.

Vera Markham took her time, lingered for a while at the back of the church, then walked slowly down the far left-hand aisle past the Lady Chapel, pausing now and again to examine the wood carvings depicting the Stations of the Cross and then, disappointed that the Lady Chapel was still engaged, collapsing finally with her shopping on a hard wooden pew. There was nothing else for it, she would simply have to wait.

Wearily, she closed her eyes (at least it was beautifully cool in here, she thought), then guiltily she remembered her formal religious training—Vera Markham hadn't been a regular church-goer since her marriage in her late teens—and got down creakily on her knees, self-consciously crossed herself, and hastily recited the Lord's Prayer. Then she sat back on the pew and began her vigil. Her thoughts drifted to her elderly mother, an averred atheist who nevertheless immediately invoked God's help the moment anything went wrong with her life and still prayed to certain saints, particularly to St. Anthony, whose attributes also included the finding of lost objects. Her mother was dreadfully forgetful now, forever losing things. . . .

Vera Markham smiled drowsily to herself. The heat of the

day and her fatigue following the morning's shopping expedition round the town were beginning to take effect. Her eyelids grew heavy, impossible to keep open a moment longer, and she drifted into a light sleep.

Almost immediately she began to dream. . . .

She was standing alone in the middle of a court-room, and there in the dock was her son Brian with his two co-defendants. Someone—a man whose voice she didn't recognise—was annoyed with her because she was withholding something which would get her Brian into a lot of trouble if the judge found out about it. There was some sort of mist, a greyish veil, around the judge; she couldn't see his face, but she was as sure as it was possible to be that it was St. Anthony. And seated on his right was an elderly woman, her mother.

Vera Markham whimpered in her sleep as she recognised the woman. She had done everything she could to keep all this from her mother, including not travelling down daily to London to attend the trial so as not to arouse her suspicions. It would kill the poor old thing to know that her only grandchild had become the innocent dupe (Vera Markham believed) in an armed London bank raid. And yet here was her mother, all worldly wise, sitting in judgment on Brian alongside St. Anthony in what was presumably the Bow Street Magistrates' Court, where the trial was being held.

This could mean only one thing, Vera Markham realised indignantly, drifting in and out of a light sleep without ever being properly awake. During one of her mother's almost daily communications with St. Anthony, he had betrayed Brian, grassed on him.

Vera Markham had never felt so affronted. Enraged, she rushed towards the bench to snatch up the judge's gavel and use it on him. Only the judge already had it in his hand and was using it himself, bringing the court to attention so that he could pass judgment.

The hammering of his gavel grew louder, the court was in uproar, then abruptly everyone fell still, the hammering ceased. Vera Markham held her breath, waited for sentence to be passed. There seemed to be some problem though, a long delay while everybody simply stood about waiting.

And then, infuriatingly, just as the judge was about to say his piece, Vera Markham woke up.

The dream left her feeling disturbed and upset, queasy in the stomach. She looked round at the Lady Chapel, but the curtain was still drawn.

Checking the time, she was amazed to find that it was nearly one-fifteen. She had been dozing for over half an hour. She really couldn't wait any longer, she decided. Besides, that dream . . . it had made her feel giddy in the head, faint. The sooner she got home and had a cup of tea and a lie-down the better. And another thing, she thought, frowning anxiously to herself. That dream was a warning, a premonition. She must tell her mother about Brian: if she didn't, somebody else would, and that would only make her mother hurt and angry with her for having left it to other people to go running to her with their tales about her grandson. It had been silly trying to keep the truth from her mother. . . . She would go round and see her this afternoon, as soon as she had had a rest. Make a clean breast of everything.

Sighing, she got up and gathered her things together. Then she inched her way awkwardly along the narrow space between the pews and into the side aisle. Pausing for a moment, she gazed longingly at the Lady Chapel, but stare as she might, the curtain refused to budge an inch.

As she started back up the aisle, her bulging shopping bags accidentally brushed against the heavy curtain screening off the Lady Chapel and dragged it along with her. She realised what had happened almost instantly and quickly freed the curtain, hoped she hadn't disturbed the person praying within. Her carelessness made her cross with herself, and she very nearly apologised out loud for it. Then she looked back and saw that the curtain had been drawn slightly open, leaving a gap between the curtain and the stone pillar of approximately eight to twelve inches which meant that anyone passing that spot could look straight into the Lady Chapel.

Dismayed, Vera Markham put down her bags and reached out for the curtain to draw it back to the pillar again. She would try to do it very quietly, wouldn't speak—apologise—not unless someone spoke to her first.

As her fingers closed round the bulky thickness of the curtain, there was a peculiar heaviness in the pit of her stomach, something like the terrible sinking feeling she had experienced the night the police had knocked on her front door about Brian.

There was something not quite right here. She sensed it instinctively. *Something was wrong.* . . .

Vera Markham's heart thudded dully. Carefully she drew back the curtain.

She looked at the altar.

Then at the woman lying before it.

The woman was on her back, so it would not have been correct to say that she had prostrated herself submissively before the altar—Vera Markham's first thoughts. The woman's hands were neatly crossed on her breast, and thrusting upwards out of the V made by her hands was a thin stick, a fine wooden stake, which appeared to be embedded deep in her chest. Her long-sleeved, pearl-grey blouse was unbuttoned and parted wide and hanging outside her skirt.

Vera Markham's gaze travelled back and forth between the altar and the first of the three short wooden pews in the Lady Chapel. A ladies' navy-blue handbag waited upright on the second pew.

Vera Markham looked back at the woman, tried to understand what had happened, what all this meant. She was too stunned to move and go right in and look at the woman close to; she couldn't even be completely sure that the woman was dead and wasn't engaged in some bizarre ritual and in a trancelike state, a coma. Somehow Vera Markham didn't think the woman was alive. Not once in all the time that she had been looking at her had she seen the woman's chest rise and fall as she breathed in and out.

Again Vera Markham looked at the handbag, then at the

purple velvet kneeler and the back of the first pew where presumably the woman would have rested her arms while she had kneeled and prayed. She continued to look at these things, as if trying to make some sense of what she was seeing, her gaze occasionally straying to the grisly sight on the top altar step and then switching instantly back to the starkly contrasting normalcy of a handbag left waiting on a pew for its owner to return and claim it. Then, hypnotically, she abruptly released the curtain, turned, picked up her things and then, without once faltering, walked calmly out into the bright golden sunlight. She didn't faint until she reached the bus-stop.

"Poor thing," someone murmured sympathetically. "It must be the heat."

CHAPTER 7

Miss Sayer heard all about it from Daphne Cross, Mrs. Pearson's erstwhile, reticent friend, when she went down to the Day Centre first thing next morning for her lunch ticket.

"Rubbish," said Miss Sayer. "It's her day off. That's the only reason she's not in the post office today."

"Suit yourself," said Daphne Cross with a shrug. "But it was her all the same. It was on the local news round-up on television early last night and it's in the *Sketch* this morning. You'd have known all about it if you weren't so mean and had a copy delivered every day like I do."

"Miss Holliday never went to church," said Miss Sayer dismissively.

Daphne Cross agreed with her. "Not in the village she didn't; but yesterday she went over to St. Anthony's in Gidding. You know, Gidding Cathedral. And yesterday was her day off, not today."

Miss Sayer glowered at her, paid for her lunch, and marched out without another word to anyone. She made straight for the library, a former manor house which, along with its grounds, had been left to the people of the village by its previous owner and now comprised the public lending library, some reception rooms for general hire, and the Over-Sixties Club.

There was an unusually long queue of people, mostly elderly, waiting in the reading-room for their turn to read the free copy of the Gidding *Daily Sketch*. Miss Sayer took one look in there and stormed out muttering to herself about people who had nothing better to do with their time. Her next port of call was the post-office stores. Tilly Cockburn sometimes brought the *Sketch* in with her of a morning and would

sit reading it if she wasn't terribly busy. Miss Sayer would ask
for a look at her copy.

The post-office stores were closed. Miss Sayer peered
through the glass in the door, but there was no one about.
Then she went down the side of the premises and stared at
Rose Cottage. It looked no different from any other day.

"I see you heard about Miss Holliday," said a gratingly familiar voice. "Dreadful, isn't it? Would you believe it? A stake
right through the heart!"

Miss Sayer turned. Soppy Molly Pearson with that know-it-
all Daphne Cross in tow.

"A stake through whose heart?" said Miss Sayer warily.

"Her in post office's," replied Mrs. Pearson. "Didn't Daphne
tell you?" Mrs. Pearson gazed in wonderment at her friend,
who shrugged and looked away. Then, looking back at Miss
Sayer with eyes large and round as saucers, Mrs. Pearson said,
"Someone—Big John Little, they're saying—put a stake right
through Miss Holliday's heart. . . . Yesterday lunch-time, in
Gidding Cathedral's Lady Chapel."

Miss Sayer said nothing for a moment. Then, even more
warily, as if she now more than half-suspected the other two
women of collusion and that this was a hoax, they hoped to
take a rise out of her: "Killed her, you mean?"

Daphne Cross flicked her eyes over her and snapped, "She's
hardly likely to be standing at her post-office counter selling
postage stamps with a thick wooden stake sticking out of her
bosom, is she?"

"You've not got that right, Daphne," Mrs. Pearson corrected
her friend. "It wasn't a *thick* stake: I heard it was only one of
Big John's withies . . . one of those thin willow branches he
cuts and weaves into hurdles for fencing."

Miss Sayer made a disparaging noise, waved a dismissive
hand in the air. "Big John Little never killed anybody. With or
without a withy. He'd be far too tired for anything as physical
as that. It's as much as he can do to stir himself out of that old
withy shed of his and do what the farmers pay him for and
finish off the poor dumb creatures that only get their forepaws

or a hind leg caught in their traps. And he never strays any further from the village than the alder marshes. Everybody knows that."

"Is that a fact?" said Daphne Cross coldly. "Well, *I* happen to know that once a week he goes into Gidding in that old van of his father's. On market-day. Every Thursday without fail. Eleven pounds fifty a bundle, that's what he fetches for his withies in Monks Lane Market. I've been over there and seen him with my own two eyes."

Miss Sayer looked at her. Then, hesitantly: "Rubbish."

They moved on slowly down the High Street towards the old brewery.

"Well, I can't say I'm sorry to see the back of her," said Mrs. Pearson flatly.

Miss Sayer snorted. "You'll think again, my girl, after a few bus trips back and forth into Gidding to pick up your pension."

"Oh dear," said Mrs. Pearson. "I hadn't thought about that." She looked worriedly at her friend Daphne. "What d'you think they'll do about my sister's new pension book? When I wrote off to them yesterday I said it was usually forwarded to Miss Holliday's post office. We've had that much trouble over it, and now it's sure to go astray. Perhaps I should write away again today and let them know what's happened."

"I shouldn't bother if I were you," said Daphne Cross dryly. "Sooner or later someone's bound to tell them there isn't a post office in Little Gidding any more."

"I wouldn't be so sure about that," Miss Sayer interpolated sourly, unwittingly agreeing with Daphne Cross, who was being sarcastic.

Reaching Fitzsimmons' Brewery, they turned left down a narrow lane and then continued on to the Day Centre for their lunch. Fish and two veg. with trifle and custard to follow. Miss Sayer hoped the fish wouldn't be greasy. Last Friday's haddock had been swimming in fat and had given her a nasty bilious attack.

Throughout lunch she was unusually quiet, though only one person noticed. Everyone else was too busy discussing the sud-

den demise of their postmistress. Nobody seemed unduly disturbed by the macabre circumstances in which Miss Holliday
had apparently died, the conversation during the meal center-
ing mainly on whether Big John Little had really had a hand
in her murder. Most thought it more than likely. "You can only
push some people so far," said Colonel Billingsley, one of the
few retired males in the village brave enough to attend the
widow-dominated Day Centre regularly and nimble enough to
sidestep the persistent reminders he got not to forget to call
round for "that glass of sherry and a piece of cake." In the colonel's opinion, Miss Holliday had asked for it where Big John
was concerned. It was a miracle the man hadn't done her in
ages ago.

A sea of nodding heads indicated that everyone agreed with
him. Including Miss Sayer, though she gave no hint of it. Her
thoughts had moved on. Sitting around speculating was just a
waste of time. Useless. What she wanted was the facts. And
she planned to get them.

There was a whist drive at the Over-Sixties Club every Friday afternoon, but today Miss Sayer begged off. She had one
of her bilious headaches coming on, she said.

"Making a special trip into town to get some aspirin, no
doubt," observed Daphne Cross when, not half an hour later,
she and Mrs. Pearson, who were on their way with Colonel
Billingsley to the Over-Sixties Club for the whist drive, spotted
the old lady scrambling aboard the bus for Gidding.

"Oh, do you think so?" said Mrs. Pearson anxiously. "She
could've had some of mine. I always carry a packet around
with me in case of an emergency."

"Oh really, Molly," said Daphne Cross impatiently. "Sometimes I wonder about you. Of course she's not going into Gidding for aspirin. She's off to see that nephew of hers, the one
who used to be a policeman. I could see her working it all out
in her head while we were having our lunch. I knew she'd
make some excuse about this afternoon. Lord knows what
she'd do if she didn't have those sick headaches of hers to fall
back on all the time."

They turned on to the narrow asphalt path which curved gracefully through the beautifully kept lawned gardens at the side of the library.

Mrs. Pearson frowned. "I do wish you'd say what you really mean, Daphne. I find it very difficult sometimes keeping up with you."

"So I've noticed," her friend tartly rejoined.

Jean Sayer, slim and still girlishly pretty for her fifty-two years, was holding the ladder for her husband when, glancing out of the window, she spotted the old lady hastening up their front path to the door. She groaned. "Oh no, here's trouble."

Her husband, who was painting the living-room ceiling and most of himself, paused and looked down at her. "What is it?"

"Who, you mean. Your aunt. Breathing smoke and fire about something. She's going to have a stroke one of these days."

"Well, how about letting her in before the bell has a seizure." David Sayer frowned as the old lady continued to keep her finger pressed down hard on the doorbell. "Anyone would think we're deaf."

"No, she's the one who's deaf," said Jean, moving to answer the door. "That's why she keeps her finger on the bell. She can't hear it so she thinks we can't either." She glanced back at him anxiously, without pausing. "You haven't forgotten you'd promised to do something for her, I hope."

She didn't catch her husband's reply. She opened the door and smiled. "Hullo, Auntie. How lovely to see you. Why didn't you phone and let us know you were coming?"

"Where's David?" the old lady demanded. Miss Sayer rarely directly acknowledged her niece by marriage, which Jean considered something of a compliment. It meant she didn't get on the old lady's nerves to the same extent that everyone else seemed to.

"In the living-room painting the ceiling," Jean replied.

Miss Sayer snorted, thrust her sunshade into the umbrella-stand near the door. "I've been telling him for two years that

that ceiling's needed painting. I might've known he'd wait for a heat wave before he'd do anything about it."

"Talking about me?" asked David cheerfully, wiping his paint-smeared hands on a rag as he came out of the living-room. "Something nice, I hope."

A tall, broad-shouldered man, David Sayer towered over his tiny aunt, who was obliged to look up when standing and talking to him as a small child would to an adult. She was not intimidated by his great height and breadth, however, and invariably spoke down to him as if he were a feeble-minded innocent.

Ignoring him for the moment, Miss Sayer went and stood in the living-room doorway and disapprovingly surveyed the disarray beyond.

"Well, we can't sit and talk in there," she said bluntly. "It'll have to be the kitchen."

"You'd better wash your face," Jean said to her husband in a whispered aside as they followed his aunt down the hall. "She'll only tell you to if you don't."

"What's wrong with it?" he whispered back.

His wife looked at him, shook her head and giggled.

Miss Sayer indicated that she wanted a cup of tea, and Jean obediently put the kettle on. Drawing out a chair, Miss Sayer sat down, then gestured to her nephew to do likewise.

"Well, Auntie," he said, sitting down opposite her. He folded his arms on the table and then leaned forward heavily on them. "To what do we owe this unexpected pleasure?"

"You know very well why I'm here," she retorted.

"Haven't a clue," he assured her with a breezy smile.

Jean mouthed "Mae Holliday" at him as she set out the cups and saucers, but he deliberately ignored her.

Miss Sayer made an impatient gesture with her hand. "The older you get, the sillier you become." She looked at him, eyes narrowed balefully. "I came over here to get away from that sort of stupidity. I couldn't get much sense out of anyone back in the village either. They're all so sure Big John Little did it. It's like listening to a worn out gramophone record."

David looked at her. "What did Big John do?"

"Killed her, murdered Mae Holliday . . . Little Gidding's postmistress."

He looked startled. "The villagers are saying that?"

"I just said so, didn't I?" she snapped. "Well?" she demanded. "Is it true?"

"I wouldn't know, Auntie," he said.

"But it is true that Mae Holliday is dead?"

"That's what it said in the *Sketch* this morning," he replied.

"Never mind the *Sketch*," she said irritably. "What do the Gidding police say?"

"How would I know?" he asked, widening his eyes at her. She snorted. "Everybody knows you live in their pockets."

Jean glanced quickly at her husband, saw the annoyed look on his face, and frowned a warning at him not to antagonise the old lady. Then she said lightly, "You probably know more about it than we do, Auntie. We only know what we read in the paper this morning, and that isn't much. There were only a few lines about it. Just that a woman who's been identified as Miss Mae Holliday was found murdered soon after lunch yesterday in the Lady Chapel of the cathedral, St. Anthony's."

Miss Sayer was quiet for a moment. Then: "What about the stake through her heart?"

Jean said, "We've heard the rumours—there's another one going round that it was a rabbit punch, or something of the sort, on the back of Miss Holliday's head that killed her—but there was nothing in the *Sketch* about how she died."

Miss Sayer's eyes narrowed thoughtfully. "Did it say whether anyone was helping the police with their inquiries?"

Jean shook her head. "There was only a very short paragraph of no more than four or five lines about it . . . in that column down the side of the front page where they print last-minute news items. You can read it for yourself, if you like. It's buried somewhere under all the painting mess in the living-room."

"Sorry," said David, looking wide-eyed at his aunt. "I used the front page to stand the paint tins on. It'll be a bit mucky."

Miss Sayer gave him a look, but all she said was, "Hmm." She peered into the tin of sweet biscuits Jean offered her, then waved it away without helping herself to anything. David and his wife exchanged glances, waited. They recognised the signs. The old lady was still getting round to telling them why she had called. Though it undoubtedly concerned Mae Holliday's murder.

"Pity," she said at length.

"About the front page of the newspaper, or that Mae Holliday has met with an untimely end?" David inquired dryly.

His aunt ignored the sarcasm. She was completely insensitive to it, anyway.

Her hooded eyelids lowered a fraction. "She was consulting —if that's the word for it—your girl-friend."

David's eyebrows rose. "My girl-friend?"

"The crystal ball gazer."

"Mrs. Charles, you mean?" asked Jean.

Miss Sayer ignored her.

"How do you know that?" David asked his aunt, and Jean could see that she was now effectively excluded from the conversation; she might as well be a fly on the wall for all the notice they would take of her.

"I saw Mae Holliday calling on her on Wednesday afternoon. She was with her for almost two hours."

"Why couldn't it have been on official post-office business?" David asked.

"Don't talk daft," said his aunt irritably. "Since when did Mae Holliday ever put herself out for anyone?"

David said, "So maybe she and Mrs. Charles were good friends."

"Hah! Don't make me laugh," said the old lady. "Mae Holliday didn't have any friends: she never wanted to be friendly with anybody. Even Agatha Dunphie, who never had a bad word to say against anyone, would tell you that if she were here today."

"All right then," said David. "She was one of Mrs. Charles's clients. There's no law against that."

"No," Miss Sayer conceded after a slight pause. She indicated to Jean that she was still waiting for her tea. Then: "She went to see Mrs. Charles about Jocelyn Smith, the superintendent of St. Anthony's Village. She thought she was going to marry him."

"Only thought?" said David wryly.

The old lady snorted softly. "I soon put a spoke in her wheel, didn't I?" Her eyes widened challengingly. "Mae Holliday charged with the care and well-being of the elderly and infirm? *Hah!*" she said derisively. "Not if I could help it! She was totally unsuitable, as I told Helena Winfield—that friend of mine who lives in St. Anthony's Village—when I was talking to her on the phone the other afternoon."

"You didn't tell her that Mae Holliday was consulting Mrs. Charles?" David said quickly.

"And why not, may I ask?" The old lady drew in her chin self-righteously. "Someone had to warn Mr. Smith about the kind of woman he was involved with. He certainly couldn't see it for himself. Helena's said often enough that he's too nice for his own good."

David shook his head. "You're going to get someone into an awful lot of trouble one day, Auntie. You've got no right to interfere in other people's lives like that, not when you don't know all the facts."

"No right?" Miss Sayer was most indignant. "My name on St. Anthony's housing list gives me every right to a say in who'll take care of me in my dotage. And it wasn't going to be Mae Holliday. I'd had as much from that woman as I was going to take."

David frowned. "You've applied for one of St. Anthony's bungalows?"

His aunt shrugged. "My name's not actually on the list yet; but I've talked it over with Helena, and she's going to put in a good word for me. She's got some influence with one or two people in high places on the church board. They've a huge waiting list, you know. I'd be on my second set of wings if I waited and went through normal channels. I'm not getting any younger, you know."

"The only way you'll ever leave the village, your cottage, is feet first," said David. "And you know it."

Miss Sayer sipped her tea, made no comment.

Her nephew leaned back in his chair, regarded her coldly. "So I suppose it's all round St. Anthony's Village that the super's intended—if that is indeed what she was—consulted fortune-tellers."

The lines round Miss Sayer's mouth set hard, her eyelids drooped. "You'd do well to read your Bible a little more often, my boy. That sort of thing is a blasphemy. A good Christian—which Mae Holliday clearly wasn't—wouldn't dream of consulting a fortune-teller."

"You really are becoming a very dangerous old woman," said David sharply, and his wife looked at him quickly, startled. She had never heard him speak to his aunt like this before. And mean what he said.

"You'll cost someone their life one of these days with your malicious tittle-tattle," he continued. He shook his head in exasperation. "You don't even bother to get your facts straight first."

Miss Sayer narrowed her eyes at him. "You know your trouble, don't you? You're like everybody else today. You've gone soft. You think every story should have a happy ending. Well, let me tell you this, my boy," she said, jabbing a forefinger at him. "This dangerous old woman, as you call me, knows life and she knows people. Mae Holliday had a rotten core, and there'll be dancing in the village streets now that she's gone. And you needn't look so shocked. Those are Big John Little's words, not mine. But murderer or not, if he leads the dancing tonight, I'll be right there alongside him; and so will everyone else in the village."

Miss Sayer had risen. Her chair scraped noisily along the floor as she pushed it back under the table.

"And while this dangerous old woman is about it," she went on imperiously, "I'll tell you something else for free—you and those namby-pamby social workers they've got here in Gidding posing as a police force. That lazy layabout with all the hair who's moved in down the road from me . . . he's up to no good either. Raphael Curry my eye! Rafeek, more like!"

Jean and David gazed wide-eyed at one another as Miss Sayer stormed out of the house.

"What did she mean by that—*Rafeek?*" asked Jean, wincing as the front door slammed shut behind the old lady. "It's a Muslim name, isn't it?"

David shrugged. "You know what she's like: she's prejudiced about everything and everyone, particularly foreigners and especially anyone with what she considers to be an abnormal amount of dark, curly body hair."

Jean looked worried. "You've really upset her; you know that, don't you?"

"Good," he said absently.

Jean watched him for a moment. Then, as she started to tidy up the tea-things: "You'll wash your face before you go out, won't you?"

"What?" He frowned at her. "I haven't finished the painting yet. Who said I was going out? I'm not going anywhere."

"Aren't you?" she asked with a small, thoughtful smile.

CHAPTER 8

Miss Sayer had a light evening meal and got it out of the way early. She was not in the least bit upset by her visit to see her nephew that afternoon, and had been nowhere near as affronted by his plain speaking as she had pretended to be when taking her leave of him. A little name-calling never hurt anyone, not when it was in a good cause. . . .

She smiled to herself. She knew how to handle David: she had learnt the secret of that years ago. All in all it had been a very satisfactory afternoon's work from her point of view. The groundwork had been laid, now all she had to do was to sit back and await results.

She angled her chair in the bay window so that it was facing the general direction of the motorway. The last thing David would want to do would be to drive through the village. That would mean his having to pass her front door to reach Edwina Charles's bungalow. He would come round the other way, via the motorway.

Miss Sayer's eyelids drooped heavily. He thought he could outsmart her, did he? A sly smile crossed her face. She could still teach him a trick or two!

Her grandmother's opera-glasses stood waiting at arm's length on the low occasional table beside her chair. She picked them up and looked through them. She wouldn't be able to see the motorway itself—that wasn't possible from her cottage—but she ought to be able to see a small section of the slip-road. She adjusted the position of her chair, looked through the glasses again. Yes, that was much better. . . .

The minutes ticked by. She began to get bored, laid the glasses in her lap, and squirmed round and squinted at the ormolu carriage clock on the mantelpiece. Eight forty-five. And it was beginning to get dark. Soon she wouldn't be able to see anything out there. It occurred to her that she might have been overly optimistic. David would come, but maybe not until tomorrow now.

She was mentally rearranging the following day's activities in anticipation of this possibility when the telephone rang. She ignored it and stuck to her post. She knew who it was: her friend, Helena Winfield, wanting a progress report. Silly cat, Miss Sayer thought irritably. She'd told Helena she would phone her as soon as she knew for certain that her plan had worked and David was going to see Edwina Charles about Mae Holliday. . . .

The old lady frowned meditatively. It could be tricky finding out what David and Edwina Charles talked about when he called on her. Though David was sure to tell Jean and Jean should be no problem. Not after what had happened this afternoon. Jean would be on the phone first thing in the morning making the peace (it might even have been her phoning a short while ago). Miss Sayer made a small, contemptuous snorting noise. Her nephew's wife didn't seem to realise that with four brothers older than herself, none of whom had made any concession to her on account of her sex or size, she (Miss Sayer) had been at loggerheads with one male member of her family or another since early infancy and had consequently developed the tough protective plating of an armadillo. Nobody could get under her skin where it hurt. A mild irritation was about the worst harm anyone could really inflict upon her.

She suddenly shot forward in her seat with her eyes glued to the opera-glasses. She had spotted someone moving stealthily along the hedgerows. My God, she thought as she realised who it was. One of these days Stan North was really going to stumble on some nature in the raw!

Her gaze moved on further up the road. Mr. Curry was outside working in his greenhouse. Now that, she thought, was typical. Almost nine o'clock at night before the lazy wretch finally decided to get up off his big fat backside and do some

real work. Still, that was the foreigner, wasn't it? she told herself. She'd seen it all before. She gave a tiny snort of disgust.
These people spent all day inside, dozy as dormice, then somewhere around nine or ten o'clock at night (in Mr. Curry's case)
they would suddenly spring to life and start digging frantically
in the garden or bang nails or what have you into loose gutter-
ing and roofing tiles, or begin tinkering about with their cars.
Just when everybody else was trying to get off to sleep. This
was the only time they seemed to get visitors too. Halfway
through the night, when everyone else had gone to bed. Like
Mr. Curry. . . . His visitors had woken her up often enough,
slamming car doors and revving up their engines when they
were leaving. Not to mention talking and laughing at the top
of their voices. . . .

Mr. Curry suddenly straightened up and came out of the
greenhouse and went indoors. He was probably missing that
big armchair he spent most of the morning lounging about in,
Miss Sayer thought cynically. She was surprised he hadn't
taken it outside into the greenhouse with him.

Her gaze moved on.

Still no sign of David.

It had grown noticeably darker in the past few minutes. And
it was almost time for her supper. Miss Sayer ate heartily immediately before retiring to her bed; otherwise she couldn't
sleep a wink. Or so she claimed.

Suddenly she saw it: a speck of bright yellow creeping
slowly down the higher reaches of the winding slip-road from
the motorway. It could have been some car other than her
nephew's, but she never for one moment doubted that it was
his.

She got up and put away the glasses for the night. It had
been a rewarding evening. And the best part of it was that she
wouldn't have to give up any of the activities she had planned
for the following day. She could make her cocoa and sand-
wiches now. But first she'd phone Helena. . . .

David was still searching in the half-light for the doorbell
when the door suddenly opened and the clairvoyante spoke.

Mrs. Charles smiled at the expression on his face.

"You really take me by surprise sometimes, Madame," he confessed ruefully. "You give the impression that you've been expecting me, and yet I didn't know I was coming here until I suddenly found myself turning off the motorway and I realised where I was. I actually meant to phone you in the morning."

"About Miss Holliday?"

He looked at her, and she smiled again at his bemused expression. "Rafe Curry—that new neighbour of your aunt's and mine—told me your aunt saw Miss Holliday visit me on Wednesday afternoon."

"Incredible," he said as they went through to the sitting-room and sat down, he on the chintz-covered sofa and the clairvoyante in a reproduction mid-Victorian button-back leather armchair. "Everybody's watching everybody else! My aunt's watching you—or rather, Miss Holliday—and Curry's watching my aunt. It would drive me up the wall living over here. I don't know how you can be so good-humoured about it. It wouldn't be so bad if my aunt weren't so dangerous with it," he went on in an aggrieved voice. "Some of the things she says about people—with no justification whatever, I might add— would make a slander lawyer rub his hands in glee."

"I wouldn't be too hard on her," said Mrs. Charles with a small smile. "I understand from Mr. Curry that Big John Little was equally interested in Miss Holliday's comings and goings on Wednesday afternoon."

David gave her an odd look. "What d'you mean?"

"Big John was fitting a new withy hurdle in the side fence of that pair of farm cottages across the road from Mr. Curry; and when he, Big John, saw Miss Holliday walking down the road, he apparently downed tools and watched her instead. That is, according to Mr. Curry's account of events. Mr. Curry appears to have been some sort of sidelines spectator to all of this," she said with another small smile. "I suspect that Stan North would've seen Miss Holliday too. The village weather man," she explained when David looked at her blankly. "He was foraging about in the wood at the bottom of my garden when she called." The clairvoyante paused, and whereas previously her tone had been light and amused, when she continued it was dry and weary, as if all of a sudden the conversation had become rather tiresome, a bore. "So it's no big secret really that Miss Holliday was here on Wednesday afternoon, should you be worried that the Gidding police will find out about it and wish to make something of it. Or am I being naïve there? Perhaps they already know that Miss Holliday consulted me on Wednesday afternoon."

"So she was a client," he said, conscious of her shift in attitude, but determined not to be put off by it.

She gave him a wide-eyed look. "Didn't your aunt tell you?"

"Well, something of the sort," he admitted with a crooked smile. "What she actually said was that Miss Holliday wouldn't have called here on post-office business."

Mrs. Charles smiled a little, and some of the tension of a moment or two earlier evaporated. "Have you spoken to the Gidding police about Miss Holliday's murder?" she inquired.

He nodded. "I called in to see them before coming over here. But your name wasn't mentioned," he said quickly. "As far as I'm concerned, they know nothing of your relationship with the woman. I was rather hoping to persuade you to volunteer that information yourself."

"Why?" she asked curiously.

He looked at her for a moment. Then: "Maybe it's wishful thinking and I'm the one who's being naïve, but I was rather hoping that it wasn't Big John who killed Mae Holliday. They're out with dogs now, you know, tracking him down. The poor devil's hiding out in the alder marshes down near the inlet where he cuts the willow branches for his withy hurdles. It could be days, weeks, before they find him."

"You say you hope he didn't kill her. Does that mean you think he's innocent?"

He shook his head. "Sadly, no. I'm inclined to agree with the Gidding lads that he's their man. He went missing from his pitch in Monks Lane Market around noon yesterday and was seen soon afterwards in St. Anthony's Square near the cathedral steps and then, a short while later, in the Bishop's Mitre—

the pub across the square from Monks Lane. One of the other Monks Lane stall-holders said Big John was in a belligerent mood all morning, aggressive, didn't want to talk to anyone, and disappeared earlier than usual for lunch and didn't come back in the afternoon. The stall-holder wasn't sure if Big John had sold all his withies or not. Big John makes his sales pitch from the rear of his van, then when he's sold out, or decided he's had enough for one day, he simply closes the rear doors and drives off. The other stall-holders never have much to do with him. . . . Too frightened to, I guess. When I was a lad, I used to be terrified of him. There's only a year or two between us, but he was—and still is, as you know—such a hulking great brute of a fellow. I used to go into a blue funk every time I spotted him . . . go miles out of my way to avoid running into him. And then one day my grandfather—Miss Sayer's father— who, as you probably know, was the village doctor, took me on one side and explained that Big John was probably far more scared of me, the village doctor's grandson, than I was of him. One of life's poor unfortunates, my grandfather called him. Someone to be pitied, not feared. And that's what I'm trying to do now, show a little pity, despite all the evidence against him." David's eyebrows rose. "I suppose you know he publicly threatened Miss Holliday, called her a witch."

"And challenged her to a fist fight," said Mrs. Charles dryly, "on at least two occasions to my certain knowledge." Her eyes widened. "Surely the Gidding police aren't taking any of this seriously? Nobody in the village did—including, I should've thought, Miss Holliday."

"Ah, but do you know *why* he threatened her?"

"No," Mrs. Charles admitted. "There was a rumour going around at one time concerning a pension he should've been receiving from the State."

David was nodding. "I know people call Big John the village layabout—none more often than my aunt—but Big John is actually entitled to an invalid pension. Only he doesn't get it, because Miss Holliday, unlike Agatha Dunphie, refused to take care of all the paperwork for him. He can't read or write, you know—none of the Littles can—and Big John's too proud to admit it to anyone. So the poor devil goes without his pension, his rightful entitlement, and scratches out a living for himself and his old dad by making withy hurdles and selling bundles of withies over in Gidding at Monks Lane Market, and from doing the odd handyman's job here and there for the villagers and local farmers. Agatha Dunphie knew the Littles couldn't read and write, so did Miss Holliday. One cared enough to pretend that she knew nothing of their disability and that it was her place to do all the necessary paperwork for them; the other didn't give a damn. And there's no way you'd ever get Big John to go over to the Department of Social Security in Gidding and ask them for help for himself and his old dad because neither of them can read nor write. So you see, for nigh on ten years now, ever since old Miss Dunphie died, Big John's been slowly coming up to the boil about Mae Holliday."

The clairvoyante gave him a bemused look. "And all of a sudden the pot boils over, he sharpens the tip of one of his withies to a fine point, lures Miss Holliday over to Gidding Cathedral, and there murders her by driving a withy stake through her heart?" Mrs. Charles paused, eyed him speculatively. "That is what happened, isn't it?"

"Who told you that?"

"You'd like me to make a list?" she asked wryly. "My brother, Cyril. He was first. He heard it down at the Black Swan late last night when he called in for a drink. Next came the postman early this morning with his version. And after him, Mr. Curry . . . though he only called to me from a distance; we didn't discuss the matter face to face. Oh, and then there was Stan North when he knocked on my door soon after lunch today wanting to know if I'd mind if he spent some more time in the wood again this afternoon. Admittedly, he said nothing about Big John and had only heard a rumour that Miss Holliday had been murdered."

"I'm sorry I asked," said David.

"Well?" she said. "Is it true?"

"Yes and no. Yes, she was found with one of Big John's

withies sticking out of her chest; and no, that wasn't what killed her. She was already dead when she was stabbed—the pathologist says—with the withy stake. It was a sharp blow to the back of the head with the hand. A kind of karate chop—the short, sharp physical blow Big John is known to use to put a netted or trapped, maimed animal out of its misery."

"Out of compassion," said the clairvoyante, so softly that David had to beg her pardon and ask her to repeat herself. Instead, she gave him a strange look. In her mind's eye, she could see Mae Holliday rising from the sofa and then coming forward and drawing back her hair to show her a non-existent scar from an imaginary head wound.

"On the right-hand side close to the ear and just below the hair-line," she murmured.

David looked at her thoughtfully. Then he nodded and said, "Yes, give or take a few centimetres. But how do you know that? The police haven't released this information to the general public yet. It's only just been confirmed by the pathologist."

The clairvoyante was quiet for a moment. Then, with a small frown: "You're not going to believe this, Superintendent: Mae Holliday herself described the head injury to me when she was here on Wednesday afternoon." She waved her hand dismissively. "And don't ask me to explain it. I don't understand it myself, any more than I can understand why Big John Little would kill somebody he openly and actively disliked—in fact hated—compassionately. Stabbing her viciously to death with a withy stake . . . yes, that does make sense; I could understand that, I could even picture him committing the act. The other way—" She shook her head slowly. "No. I simply can't see it myself. So if that's why you're here, you're looking for quick answers to questions which for the most part I find totally incomprehensible, then I'm afraid I can't be of any help at all to you."

"But you know why she came to see you."

"Yes."

"And you're not going to say why she was seeing you?"

The clairvoyante shook her head. "For the moment, no. Perhaps never, depending on whether or not I think her visit here on Wednesday had any bearing on her murder. And from what you've told me, it wouldn't seem that it had."

David curbed his annoyance at her refusal to confide in him and tried an indirect approach, though he did not really expect it to prove any more successful and would have been disappointed in a way if it were. It was the thing he liked most about her. Her complete integrity where her clients were concerned.

"Mae Holliday was keeping steady company with a gentleman. Did she tell you that?"

"No. She made no mention of a man-friend."

The crooked smile was back again. "So my aunt was wrong there," he said. "Aunt Margaret was of the opinion that Mae Holliday feared a proposal of marriage might not have been forthcoming from her lover."

"Mae Holliday didn't come to me to cross my palm with silver and have her fortune told, if that's what you and your aunt are thinking." The clairvoyante hesitated, smiled faintly. Then: "May I know the name of Miss Holliday's gentleman friend?"

"You may. It'll be in all the papers tomorrow, anyway. Jocelyn Smith, the resident superintendent of St. Anthony's Village—a kind of old people's home for women only. I don't know if you know the place. It's a small, purpose-built village of one-bedroom bungalows in a rather pretty landscaped garden setting in South Gidding. Owned and administered by the Church, of course. Smith's a good few years older than she was. Looks it, anyway. He's taken the news very hard. He appears to have been genuinely fond of her. Apparently, he saw qualities in her that no one else could see."

"I'm sure she had them."

The ex-Detective Chief Superintendent of Police gazed intently at the clairvoyante, but he couldn't make up his mind if she were being serious or not.

"You're absolutely certain that nothing Mae Holliday had to

say to you when she called here on Wednesday has any bearing on her murder?"

The clairvoyante looked at him gravely. "You must find some way of salving your conscience over Big John other than through me, Superintendent."

"Oh," he said. Then, with a rueful smile: "You didn't like my story about my grandfather?"

"It had a certain ring of truth to it. However, I thought it rather more likely that you would have some other, more definite reason for feeling guilty about Big John. And you are feeling guilty about something, Superintendent," said the clairvoyante, smiling fleetingly. She paused. Then, gently: "I'm quite sure that this is not the first time the poor man has fallen foul of the law. He is, as your grandfather said of him, one of life's poor unfortunates."

David was silent for a moment or two. Then, frowning: "You weren't living in the village before it had a grocery store, were you?"

She shook her head.

He went on: "Big John allegedly stole some groceries from the van which used to call here once a week. At least this was what the van driver claimed. He wasn't the regular man: he was only filling in for a month or two while the other chap was off sick. A young constable went round to have a word with Big John about the missing groceries, and Big John pulled his withy knife on him and threatened to kill him. And then Big John did what he always does when the going gets a little rough. He scarpered into the alder marshes and laid low. It unfortunately fell down to me to issue the order for him to be brought in. Dogs were used that time too, and I was actually there on the spot when they finally cornered him."

David frowned again, paused. "I'll never forget the look on his face. He wasn't terrified, as some people might suppose. He was too proud for that. It was a kind of resigned despair, a terrible hopelessness. Pathetic. I've been against blood sports from that day to this. I can't think about hare-coursing or fox-hunting without seeing the look on Big John's face that day."

"I take it he didn't steal the groceries."

David sighed softly. "The relief driver's home looked like a grocery warehouse when we checked it. He knew Big John was a bit simple and would probably do something stupid and make things look worse for himself, and he simply used the poor wretch for his own ends. So like you said, Madame . . . I owe Big John one. And I apologise for making it seem as though I wanted you to make things good for me with him."

Mrs. Charles said, "I would honestly like to help you, but I don't see how I can. I assure you, from what you've told me, there's nothing to suggest that Miss Holliday's visit here on Wednesday had anything to do with her murder. Her reason for coming to see me was of an extremely personal and delicate nature, and her death does not release me from my obligation to respect the trust she placed in me by seeking my advice. Quite the reverse. In this particular instance, I am even more bound by my client's death to respect her confidence."

David looked at her. "But *why*, Madame? *How* could Big John lure, as you put it, Mae Holliday over to Gidding Cathedral to meet him when it was more than she could do to pick up a pen and fill in a few simple forms for him? I've been listening to my aunt moan about that woman for the last ten years, and Mae Holliday, to me, is like the well-known television personality you bump into unexpectedly in the street or supermarket and greet like an old friend, without thinking, because they've spent so much time in your home by way of the TV screen that you feel you've known them all your life. I've known Mae Holliday for years without ever having met her. And I say there's no way she would've gone over to Gidding on Big John's account. Or on anybody else's, for that matter."

CHAPTER 9

The clairvoyante nodded her head. "I agree with you. Mae Holliday wouldn't have gone into Gidding on anyone's account other than her own, or on post-office business."

She hesitated. Then, thoughtfully: "Thursday is Gidding's market-day: people converge on the town from all round—there's even a special bus service in the village on market-day which collects passengers at the post-office stores at ten-thirty in the morning and then picks them up at a certain prearranged spot near St. Anthony's Square at three-thirty in the afternoon for the return trip. I doubt that Miss Holliday would've availed herself of this service yesterday—she has her own transport. But why are you so sure that she went into Gidding to meet someone? What makes you think she wasn't over there on a simple, straightforward shopping excursion like anyone else who makes a trip into Gidding on market-day?—which, incidentally, also happens to have been her day off. I shouldn't have thought there'd be many people who make a trip into town on market-day who wouldn't include a visit to the Monks Lane Market on their shopping itinerary. Surely, then, it isn't inconceivable that Big John simply saw Miss Holliday in Monks Lane and followed her to St. Anthony's?"

"Why would Mae Holliday want to go there specifically—into Gidding Cathedral, of all places?"

"I thought people usually went to church to pray," Mrs. Charles replied evenly. Her eyes widened. "And St. Anthony is the patron saint of lovers and marriage, Superintendent. Or perhaps she sought merely to sit quietly for a time and meditate."

"Did she have some reason for wanting to meditate?"

The clairvoyante smiled at his persistence. "Possibly. This personal problem of hers was becoming obsessive. I also think it's possible that the nature of her problem was such that she might've wished to seek specific help from Our Lady with it," she said in anticipation of David's next question.

"Mae Holliday never went to church. I remember my aunt saying so on many occasions."

"That doesn't necessarily make Miss Holliday a disbeliever," said Mrs. Charles quietly.

David thought for a moment. "Could it—her reason for wanting to pray specifically in the Lady Chapel—have anything to do with her wanting to make some kind of confession . . . the sort she might prefer not to make to a priest—a man?"

"Really, Superintendent," said Mrs. Charles with a mildly reproving frown. "You don't seriously expect me to answer that question, do you?"

"No," he said after a small pause. "But I would like you to convince me that this was what she was really doing in Gidding Cathedral—merely praying, or meditating—and that she didn't go there to meet someone. I agree with you that Big John probably spotted her in Monks Lane Market and simply followed her into the cathedral; I am utterly convinced, however—and so are the police—that if such were the case, then it was quite by chance. There was nothing prearranged between them, nothing premeditated about her murder. It's almost certain that Big John would've been primed with drink—I don't think I've ever seen him completely sober . . . latterly, that is—therefore, *if* he killed her, he did so, quite simply, in the heat of the moment and while under the influence of alcohol."

David leaned forward slightly. "But what was she doing in the cathedral in the first place? That's what I'd like to know. Did she go there to pray because she had something on her mind which was deeply distressing her and she wished to pray or meditate about it; or was she there to meet someone? (And I'm talking now about someone other than Big John.) Either or, Madame? Or both?"

"I don't know, Superintendent," she said, slowly shaking her head.

He relaxed back again, folded his arms, regarded her contemplatively. "Shall I tell you what the Gidding police and I think? We think Mae Holliday was a witch, mixed up in one of these Satanist black magic cults that are flourishing up and down the country at the moment. And I personally think that this was why she came to you on Wednesday and that this was what she was doing in the Lady Chapel the next day. I think she was terrified out of her wits. Someone was threatening her life (someone other than Big John, who was long on words and short on action—a point, incidentally, on which the police and I strongly disagree). That someone, Madame, I believe lives here in the village—which, as you doubtless know, is rumoured to have had strong links in the past with witchcraft—and Mae Holliday came to you, someone familiar with the occult and occult practices, in the hope that you could perhaps allay her fears. I can even conceive of the possibility that she went to the Lady Chapel, under instructions perhaps from the leader of the coven to which she belonged, to perform some special black magic rite in concert with some other party, and either by design or accident, something happened between them— they argued, quarrelled—and she finished up dead."

The clairvoyante looked at him steadily. "I always understood it was vampires, not witches, who were staked through the heart."

"True," he said. "However, you can forget about the stake; that's not influencing anybody's thinking here. It's the reel of film the police found in the hip-pocket of her skirt. . . . A very amateurish home-made movie," he added. Then, when the clairvoyante remained silent: "It appears to have been made about twenty years ago, judging by the type of film used."

"Go on," she said when he paused. "I assume you've seen what was on the film."

"Yes. Clive Merton ran it through for me tonight before I came here. It's only about a minute and a half long. And as I've said, all in all it's a pretty amateurish effort. Jerks and jumps about all over the place, and the lighting is extremely poor; in fact, I very much doubt that the cameraman bothered with any artificial lighting at all. It appears to be a recording of some kind of black magic ritual. There hasn't been time as yet to call in any of the experts in the field for their opinion on it; and depending on how secret the rite is, maybe it'll be one they know nothing about. The first scene is of a child—a fair-haired girl of about ten or twelve dressed in a long white robe —lying dead in a coffin. Not a real coffin. Somebody has knocked one together—out of cheap plywood, by the looks of it —specially for the occasion. The dead child is wearing a circlet of mistletoe on her head, and her arms are crossed on her breast; and there are candles burning—four of them—at the head and foot of the coffin.

"All but the final few seconds of the film, I should perhaps mention before going any further," he interpolated abruptly, "is shot in a mock-up of a church."

He went on: "Then, suddenly, the camera shoots to the face of a large clock—one with a big face like a railway clock. The hands are at a few minutes to twelve—it's quite dark, so one would imagine it's approaching the hour of twelve midnight. Then the camera abruptly switches back to the coffin, only now it's been nailed down and the circlet of mistletoe—which was formerly on the dead child's head—has been laid on its lid the way one would normally lay a wreath of flowers. The candles have been snuffed out and are smoking. Back to the clock. Midnight. Then the next and final shot is of a huge church bell which is apparently being tolled by another child in a white hooded robe—or the same child we saw earlier in the coffin . . . it's too dark to tell—and the child's face is partially shrouded by the hood on her robe. The final scene appears to have been filmed in a genuine church. The bell was real."

"The film was shot out of sequence?"

"How do you mean?"

"If, as you've said, the child in the coffin is dead, she couldn't have tolled the church bell at the end of the film, could she?"

He waved a hand in the air. "Sorry. I should've said 'playing dead.' That's if Merton is right. He thinks it's a movie made of Mae Holliday when she was a little girl. I agree with him. So she couldn't have been dead, could she?"

Mrs. Charles looked at him thoughtfully. "Not if it was Mae Holliday who was murdered in the Lady Chapel yesterday."

"Well, there's no doubt about that," he said. "It was her all right. And she wasn't playing dead this time, I can assure you."

"Chief Superintendent Merton is quite sure about that: it was Mae Holliday?"

"Positive," he replied. "She had plenty of identification on her—all the usual stuff: driving licence, credit cards . . ." He paused and considered the clairvoyante contemplatively. Then, after a moment: "The woman who runs the village store, Tilly Cockburn, made the positive identification of the body. Merton didn't know about the boy-friend at the time. He came forward later. It was bad luck about him, actually," he said with a small frown. "He found out about it the worst possible way. Some old dear from St. Anthony's Village blurted out the news to him with all the subtlety of a power-driven sledge-hammer. I try not to think too much about her—the sweet little old lady who told him—in case I start to wonder who gave her the sad tidings. . . . A certain person not so very far distant springing immediately to mind, if you follow my meaning—" He smiled grimly.

Mrs. Charles said hesitantly, "Did the police find anything else unusual on Miss Holliday?"

David looked at her keenly. "You had something special in mind?"

She half-smiled. "So that's the way it is to be between us, is it?"

He laughed. "No. You're going to read all about it tomorrow. In her skirt-pocket, with the reel of movie-film, was a locally hand-made lace handkerchief (no mystery about that), and the cover of an old movie-star magazine with her name written on it."

"How old is old?" asked Mrs. Charles.

"Nineteen fifty-something. You know, when those magazines with all the gossip about film stars were popular."

"Anything else?"

"The reel of film was wrapped in a tatty piece of silver
paper. That any use to you?" he asked.

Mrs. Charles smiled, shook her head. "No, I don't think I
can make anything sinister out of that."

"Then how about a kid's purse?" he said, and watched the
clairvoyante's eyes closely. "One that's been cut in the shape
of a dog. . . ."

Reluctantly, David started up his car and put it in gear. That
woman, he thought, would make a marvellous poker player.
She hadn't given a thing away—possibly, he had to admit, because there was nothing *to* give away. Maybe Merton was
right and Big John did kill Mae Holliday. That too was a possibility. Time would tell.

He sighed a little. There was only one consolation. If Edwina Charles did know something that could take the heat off
Big John, even if only temporarily, she would do something
about it. He could do no more for now.

David cursed quickly under his breath. He had been so
engrossed in thought he had forgotten that he had meant to
turn round and go back home along the motorway.

"Damn," he said as he drove past the brightly illuminated
front window of his aunt's cottage. He supposed he should
stop and go in and say hello.

*And be forced to drink some of that foul-tasting cocoa she
went to bed with every night?*

No, thank you very much!

He put his foot down hard and sped on into the village. A
forlorn hope, but maybe the old girl hadn't seen him.

The clairvoyante listened to David drive away. She would
never have admitted it to his face, but the moment Rafe Curry
had mentioned Miss Sayer's interest in Mae Holliday's visit,

she had known that sooner or later David would come and see her. And knowing Miss Sayer, it would probably be sooner.

Mae Holliday's murder, thought the clairvoyante, was much like Mae Holliday herself. Confusing. A mishmash of fact and fiction.

But what was fact and what was fiction?

She had been asking herself that question ever since Mae Holliday had visited her. The restrictions which had been placed on her reading of the Tarot cards had been severely inhibiting and had revealed only one clear truth about Mae Holliday, which in itself had proved even more inhibiting. Mae Holliday was a pathological liar, to a large extent living in a fantasy world, a world of her own creation.

No, thought the clairvoyante, frowning. That wasn't quite true. Shortly before she left, Mae Holliday spoke of her fear of clocks. Especially Agatha Dunphie's broken railway clock. At the time, Mrs. Charles had been inclined to dismiss this alleged phobia as another of Mae Holliday's fantasies. But she now knew that this was not so. From what David had said of the clock in the home-made movie the police had shown him, Mae Holliday could have had every good reason for fearing clocks. That is, if she were the child acting out the part of a corpse in the movie; and the clairvoyante saw no reason to doubt the claim made by Gidding Constabulary's Chief Superintendent Merton that Mae Holliday was the child. The spotted-dog purse really existed too.

And yet the Tarot said Mae Holliday was a liar.

No. . . .

The Tarot had been much more precise. Mae Holliday was a liar, yes, but first and foremost to herself. The lies she told other people merely compounded the lies she had already told herself. Therefore when Mae Holliday told a lie, she was sinning not so much against others as against herself. . . .

But to what extent did she know that she was lying to herself?

The clairvoyante gazed reflectively into the distance.

As she had sat listening to Mae Holliday talk about herself, she had suspected that Mae Holliday knew she was lying, realised it probably for the first time in years. Up until then, she had lived happily and contentedly with the lies, never questioning them. And then suddenly something had happened. She had suffered some kind of cataclysmic shock which had revolutionised her thinking and inevitably partially reactivated that part of her brain which she had mentally blocked off. She was slowly coming out of a state of suspended animation, a form of amnesia, throughout which she had conditioned herself to live and believe a lie she had told herself many years ago, the one on which she had founded her present life, and was gradually remembering the truth.

From what David had told her, the clairvoyante was predisposed to think that the shock to Mae Holliday's system which had triggered off her remembering processes and the gradual rejection of the original lie, could have been an anticipated proposal of marriage. Marriage was no state for an amnesiac—someone like Mae Holliday who *knew* she was suffering from amnesia and had been living a lie—to enter into without first trying to fill in the blanks in one's past life. And this was really why Mae Holliday had been interested only in the past, why she had been so adamant that her future should not be read. What she had in effect been saying was that she had no intention of marrying her man-friend if she did not fully recover her memory.

But why had she preferred to hope rather than to know for certain from a complete reading of the Tarot what the outcome of her investigations would be? Had some sixth sense told her that she had no future?

The clairvoyante considered this possibility and then dismissed it. Mae Holliday had not the slightest inkling that she was about to die. And yet for all that, she had accurately described not only the way in which she would be killed—by a blow to the back of the head—but had also known the exact spot where that blow would be delivered.

Was it a subconscious premonition of something yet to come which had somehow become interwoven with the original lie she had told herself at the start of her fantasy life? Had this premonition then become part of the past instead of taking its rightful place in the future?

Or was David right?

Was Mae Holliday a witch? Had she committed some serious transgression punishable by death and been warned by someone from her coven that this was to be her fate? Was this how she had known the way in which she was to die?

David was right about one thing: witchcraft, Satanism, was on the increase. There could be a witches' coven meeting secretly either in the village or one of the neighbouring villages. Or even in Gidding.

Mrs. Charles rose and crossed to the window, picked up the wine-table which she had deliberately removed from full view when she had heard a car pull up outside and realised that she was about to be visited by David Sayer. She carried the table over to the sofa and sat down again. She had dropped a magazine casually on top of the table when she had glanced out of the window and recognised her visitor, using it to cover Mae Holliday's Tarot card reading, which the clairvoyante had left undisturbed since Mae Holliday had called on her.

There were five cards in the spread, all but two of which were lying face down. The cards which had been dealt out face down concerned the present and the future, that area of Mae Holliday's life forbidden to the clairvoyante. The other two cards, symbolic picture cards from the Major Arcana—*The Moon* and *Judgment*—represented Mae Holliday's past. *The Moon* related to the distant past, *Judgment* to the more recent past.

The clairvoyante had been re-examining these two cards moments before David had arrived. She looked at them again now in the light of the more up-to-date information he had given her.

The Moon. . . . The self-deception, the twilight life Mae Holliday had been leading because of this self-deception, her false pretenses, deceit.

And now, having regard for what David had told her . . .

The clairvoyante frowned. Yes, all of those things still applied. Nothing had changed there. But another door might possibly have opened. . . .

Somewhere in Mae Holliday's distant past someone had taken advantage of her. (*Forced her, a mere child at the time, to take part in a home-made movie of some bizarre black magic ritual?*)

It was a very strong possibility, backed up by the card representing her more recent past, *Judgment.*

Yes, definitely. . . . Someone *had* taken advantage of Mae Holliday. Unfairly.

That card, *Judgment,* also judged and condemned her for her intolerance and her unkind attitude towards other people, made clear the need for repentance, that she should change her ways.

It also suggested atonement.

Mae Holliday was going to pay for her sins—*a sin or sins against another person?* Had paid for them, the clairvoyante reminded herself. With her life.

The clairvoyante closed her eyes, let her thoughts flow freely. . . .

Someone from Mae Holliday's distant past, someone who had taken unfair advantage of her during her childhood, her formative years, had passed judgment on her and then, after many years' absence, suddenly come back into her life and sentenced her to death.

A small frown furrowed the clairvoyante's brow.

Big John Little could only be that person if he had in some way featured in Mae Holliday's distant past and known her when she was a little girl.

It was possible, of course, thought the clairvoyante. But not very likely. Though Big John, who was now being hunted by the police in connection with Mae Holliday's murder, would undoubtedly appear somewhere in her reading. . . .

Mrs. Charles gazed at the cards lying face down on the table, then slowly turned up the one which immediately followed *Judgment,* the first of the three remaining cards in Mae

Holliday's reading. This was the card which had represented the present, that short span of time through which Mae Holliday had then been passing and which, inevitably, in view of the events of the past twenty-four hours, concerned not only Mae Holliday but Big John Little as well.

It was *The Hanged Man,* the twelfth symbolic picture card in the Major Arcana.

For Mae Holliday it indicated the endeavours she was then making in her search for her real self: a suspension of time with her innermost soul laid bare to expose what was false and what was real. This had been Mae Holliday's goal; and it was a goal *The Hanged Man* forewarned might never be attained.

A shadow crossed the clairvoyante's face as she continued with the reading.

For Big John *The Hanged Man* was a prediction . . .

A life in suspension awaiting transition, the passing from one stage to another—from life to death if and when he left the sanctuary of the alder marshes.

The clairvoyante drew in a deep breath and then let it out in a soft sigh. Her hand moved on, picked up the next card, turned it over. Then, without pausing to examine it, she turned up the fifth and final card. She knew that it would be *The Devil:* she always knew when and where this particular card would appear in a reading and it was not something she could explain. There were no dramatic electric impulses as her hand made contact with it, just a quiet sureness that this card, the one she was about to deal out, was the embodiment of all that was bad and evil.

She looked now at the fourth card which she had earlier passed over without bothering to examine.

The Emperor . . . A man of some stature, certainly of great influence, who wielded immense power over Mae Holliday; a man whose influence on her was reinforced by *The Devil.* A man who held Mae Holliday's life in bondage. Very likely ever since she was a small child.

The clairvoyante thought for a moment, then looked back at *The Hanged Man* and studied it in more detail.

She would hear again from David Sayer within the next forty-eight hours. He would tell her that the search for Big John Little was over, he had been found, and that the investigation into the murder of Little Gidding's postmistress was now closed as far as the Gidding police were concerned.

Only it wasn't closed. It had never really been opened. Not properly.

CHAPTER 10

The clairvoyante did not look at the morning newspaper until after she had finished her breakfast.

The paper was late arriving, anyway. And it had Mr. Curry's name scrawled in Biro across the top of it. The new newspaper delivery boy, who had started at the beginning of the week, was still having trouble sorting everyone out. The clairvoyante and Mr. Curry shared the same taste in national morning newspapers, so assuming Mr. Curry had got her newspaper and not somebody else's, there was no real harm done. There were only five other houses along the road. Miss Sayer did not have any newspapers delivered. Mrs. Charles recalled over-hearing Miss Sayer complaining to a woman-friend about the cost of buying a newspaper today, both of whom had then gone on to declare it a senseless waste of money anyhow when one could read *all* the daily morning papers down at the library for free. So Mr. Curry had a one-in-five chance of getting the newspaper of his choice.

Mrs. Charles poured herself another cup of coffee and took it with her into the sitting-room to read the paper.

The manhunt for Mae Holliday's murderer in Little Gidding's alder marshes had taken precedence over the actual murder itself, although mention was now being made of the home-made movie which had been found in the hip-pocket of her skirt and which, the report then went on to say, was believed by the police to be connected with witchcraft. (Miss Sayer was going to love that! thought the clairvoyante wryly.)

Passing reference was also made to the child's small dog-shaped money-purse, a lace handkerchief embroidered with forget-me-nots, and the cover of an old movie-star magazine

which David Sayer had told her were found in the
postmistress' skirt-pocket along with the reel of film. It was
unclear from the newspaper report where the police had actually located these items, though a comment a little farther on
to the effect that it was not thought that anything had been
stolen from the murder victim's handbag, which was found on
a pew of the Lady Chapel, could have predisposed one to suppose that this was where the police had uncovered them.

The doorbell rang while Mrs. Charles was still reading the
report.

Rafe Curry was looking for his newspaper.

No paper had been delivered at his cottage that morning
(for the second time this week), and he wondered if the new
delivery boy had inadvertently pushed two through Mrs.
Charles's mail-slot.

He protested when Mrs. Charles explained the situation and
insisted that she should keep his newspaper; he would go
down to the newsagent in the village later in the morning, he
said, and see if he couldn't sort things out.

"No, really, I insist," said the clairvoyante. "You must take
it. I'm sure my copy will turn up sometime."

Mr. Curry followed her into the sitting-room while she got it
for him. It had turned cool overnight, and he was wearing a
thick, dark green combat jumper over his jeans. He hadn't
shaved and he looked tired, bleary-eyed. There had been a lot
of noise coming from the general direction of his cottage
around 2 A.M. that morning—car doors banging and loud talking, a woman's high-pitched laugh—which had disturbed the
clairvoyante (and everybody else in the near vicinity, she
would have thought), and this no doubt accounted for his noticeably fatigued appearance this morning.

"Looks like rain, doesn't it?" he remarked as Mrs. Charles
straightened the paper. "I've half a mind to do some gardening
today. That would really get the old girl up the road going,
wouldn't it—?" He grinned.

His grin widened as Mrs. Charles looked up at him questioningly.

"Margaret Sayer," he explained. "The old bat who lives in the cottage at the top of the road. She's been watching me through binoculars again. I've been waiting for it to rain for ages, so I can get outside in a raincoat and do something really eccentric to drive her nuts."

"You'll do that all right," said Mrs. Charles with a smile, handing him his newspaper.

"She's not got much of a sense of humour, has she?"

"I wouldn't think any at all," said the clairvoyante, going with him to the door.

"Nasty business about Sweet Mae, wasn't it?" he remarked matter-of-factly. It was the first time since the murder of their postmistress that he had met up with the clairvoyante at close enough quarters to discuss the matter properly. "Was there anything in the paper about Big John? Have they found him?"

"Not yet."

"Poor sod," said Mr. Curry. "Sweet Mae must've really got under his skin. Was it true what I heard said about her and his pension? She didn't really get it stopped, did she?"

"I wouldn't think she could," said the clairvoyante.

"Oh, I don't know," he said. "Some people see themselves as the custodians of the nation's purse-strings. And she wasn't one to let anybody put anything over her, was she?"

"She always struck me as being a reasonably intelligent woman. I think most people can see that Big John, despite his reputation for being a lazy layabout, isn't capable of earning a proper living."

"You could be right," he conceded. "But for a Yorkshire lass, she was a right cow. If you'll pardon me for saying so. They certainly ran out of salt when they got round to making her," he said with a flickering grin. "That's if it's true what they say about folk from those parts and they really are the salt of the earth."

The clairvoyante regarded him thoughtfully. "Miss Holliday came from Yorkshire?"

"*Ee-bah-gum,* she did," said Mr. Curry. "She'd put in a lot of work on her voice and got rid of most of the accent, but just occasionally when she was het up about something, she'd forget and drop her guard and her true roots would show through. I'm from Yorkshire myself," he went on. "That's probably why my ear's more sensitive to the accent of a Northerner and I picked up her occasional lapses of speech."

"You surprise me," said Mrs. Charles. "About Miss Holliday, I mean. My brother told me it said in the local paper yesterday that she came to the village from Gidding."

"Maybe she did. But before that it was from somewhere in West Yorkshire. Within a stone's throw of Leeds or Bradford—possibly Dewsbury, my home town. Take my word for it." He stepped out on to the porch and looked up at the dark grey skies with widening eyes. "Big John's going to be in a spot of bother if the weather people have got it right for once and we get those heavy thundery showers they've promised us for today. If the marshes flood and he gets caught in the wrong place at the wrong time . . ." He shrugged, left the sentence unfinished.

"I doubt that that will happen to Big John," said the clairvoyante quietly. "The alder marshes are the safest place for him. He'll be all right so long as he remains there."

"I daresay you're right. The alder marshes to him are a bit like the briar patch was to Br'er Rabbit, aren't they?" he said with a cheery wave and another grin as he started back down the path.

But there the similarity ended, thought the clairvoyante, closing the door. One was a natural-born survivor; the other wasn't.

It was raining heavily. Mrs. Charles paused momentarily on the porch to close her umbrella and shake it free of moisture, then she passed under the huge semicircular Norman arch into the church.

The day outside, after an hour of, at times, almost torrential rain, was close and muggy. Inside the church, the atmosphere was chilly, damp on the skin.

The Lady Chapel would be on her left as she entered, the

clairvoyante's brother, Cyril Forbes, had told her the previous day when he had brought her the news of Mae Holliday's murder. Cyril had taken up residence in the village of Little Gidding almost a year before his sister had moved there, and during this time he had sung in the St. Anthony's Church choir. Throughout his childhood and his teens, Cyril's singing voice had shown sufficient promise for his mother, a professional opera singer herself, to entertain the sincere hope that he would likewise choose the opera for a career. In fact, she had been quite ruthlessly determined about it and had for many years vigorously pursued this end by ensuring that he was educated at one of the more illustrious of the English cathedral public schools. Unfortunately, Cyril had shown equal determination and had ultimately pursued his own aims, which had been in an entirely different direction. The damage done to his vocal chords through years of misuse as a Punch and Judy entertainer (he claimed) led to his resignation from the church choir. Nowadays, the only singing he did was under the shower.

The church was empty, the Lady Chapel unoccupied.

Mrs. Charles's footsteps echoed round the massive church, and conscious of the noise she was making, she kept her heels off the stone-flagged floor—under which, she noted, the Bournes lay buried—and walked on tiptoe. Not many people walked in this part of the church, and the oblong burial stones with their centuries-old inscriptions were in excellent condition, easy to read.

Reaching the Lady Chapel, she paused. It was even smaller than she had imagined, approximately fourteen feet long by eight feet wide, with everything—the altar and its three wooden pews—scaled down accordingly to size. The faded heraldic standards decorating the stone walls were those, her brother had told her, of the family of the seventeenth-century nobleman, Sir Hamilton Bourne, who had built the Lady Chapel.

There was a narrow strip of rich deep-purple carpet on the wide step before the altar where Mrs. Charles assumed Mae

Holliday's body had been discovered. The carpeting looked brand-new. A small white-and-gold statuette of the Virgin Mary gazed down from a narrow alcove above the altar. The lace-edged altar cloth and silk frontal, and the altar flowers—irises—were white.

Ranged along the eastern wall and at either side of the altar was a heavy purple-and-gold brocade curtain patterned with the fleur-de-lis, the heraldic emblem of the Bourne family. The curtaining was continued for a short distance down the side walls and, according to Cyril, concealed a small studded oak door on the north wall to the left of the altar. This door was known as "the Devil's door." Cyril told his sister that it was not at all uncommon for some old churches to have such a door in their north walls which was held to be the side where the Diabolical One lurked in wait for the unwary. The Devil's door was opened at baptisms and communions to let out the Devil, Cyril explained. He also said that during the latter half of the seventeenth and the early part of the eighteenth centuries, the Lady Chapel had been permanently screened off from the main church and had been used by the Bournes exclusively for their own private devotional purposes. The Devil's door gave them their own personal means of access whereby they could come and go as they pleased and in complete privacy. Cyril understood that legend further had it that the Devil's door was never closed while the Bournes were at their prayers. He assumed the legend had grown up around the intimate dealings it was alleged one of the Bournes had once had with Satan. The rest of the family, he supposed, weren't taking any chances.

Mrs. Charles passed in front of the altar to the brocade curtain on the north wall, which Cyril had assured her concealed the Devil's door, and drew it carefully aside. The door was there with its large, clumsy-looking key in the lock. All as Cyril had said. She was surprised at the accuracy of detail in all that he had told her. Cyril was usually so vague about everything.

She tried the round, black wrought-iron handle, but the door was locked. Cyril said it gave on to a cloistered courtyard which in turn gave on to a narrow alley-way which debouched into Monks Lane. There was a free right of public access at all times to the cloisters from the alley-way, though St. Anthony's parish paper, which Cyril still received, had recently reported that the cloisters were undergoing extensive restoration work and that public access to this area was temporarily restricted. On market-day, the alley-way linking Monks Lane with the cloisters was used by some of the market traders as a dumping ground for their empty cardboard cartons and other litter which would otherwise have needlessly cluttered Monks Lane and made it an even worse obstacle course for the crowds of people who packed the lane on market-day to have to nego-tiate.

Mrs. Charles dusted her hands lightly together. The door-handle was rusted, flaking.

"So when's the big celebration?" someone—a man—asked.

She turned towards the sound of the voice.

"You're from the village—Little Gidding—aren't you?" the man went on, grinning. "I've seen you there."

He was standing with one hand clutching the heavy purple curtain which was used to screen off the Lady Chapel when it was in use. He was about thirty-five, not very tall, going bald, and was wearing a dark suit with a blue, white-collared shirt and a white tie. Mrs. Charles recognised him but let him intro-duce himself.

"Arthur Dunphie, Agatha's nephew," he said. He let go of the curtain and walked over to her. For a small man, he had an unusually heavy, flat-footed tread and a gait something like that of a stout penguin.

Mrs. Charles said, "What celebration would that be?"

"Wasn't Big John Little always going around promising ev-erybody there'd be dancing in the streets when Her Majesty Queen Mae shuffled off this mortal coil?"

Arthur Dunphie had dark brown, almost black eyes, small pointed white teeth, and a smile which could be infectious, disarming. In the present circumstances, the smile on his face

had all the warmth and charm of a steadily advancing croco-
dile, and the clairvoyante regarded him distastefully.

He laughed off her disapproval and sat down on the pew in
the front row, leaned back and crossed his legs. "Mae Holliday
hated me and I hated her. Never let it be said that I let a little
thing like murder come between such a beautiful friendship."

He waved a hand airily about him, then draped his arm casually over the back of the pew. "It beats me what a nasty girl
like her was doing in a nice place like this. Unless it's true: that
bit in the paper this morning about witchcraft."

He puffed out his cheeks and exhaled noisily through his
barely parted lips. "I spent a small fortune on a private dick
hoping I'd get lucky and he'd turn something up on her. And
what did he find? Nothing. Not a sausage! It was as though
there was no such person. . . . That's what I thought when
this birdbrain I'd hired made his report. There was nothing in
it I didn't already know, and that was precious little. If I
believed in such things, I'd say Mae was an alien from another
planet!" He slowly shook his head, spoke disgustedly. "And all
the time she had that damned film on her."

He paused and looked at Mrs. Charles searchingly, and not
for the first time. Twice now he had given her the same look,
as if he expected her to say something, make some admission,
or he was looking for something. Pointed ears and a warty
nose? she wondered wryly, recalling the dominant physical
characteristics of the wicked witch in a book of fairy tales she
had read as a child.

He folded his arms, shook his head again. "Just my rotten
luck. If only I could've laid my hands on that reel of movie-
film ten years ago . . . She'd never have got a red cent of Aunt
Agatha's money, I can tell you that," he said bitterly. "I was
sure she had some hold over the old girl—and God knows I
called her a frustrated old witch often enough. But who'd have
thought it was true, an actual fact." His neat eyebrows shot up,
and he looked again searchingly at the clairvoyante. "She really was a witch!"

His eyes narrowed fractionally and his mood changed; he

became less self-pitying and more positive. "So what happens now, I wonder? I dropped into the village store on my way over here, but Tilly didn't seem to know anything—y'know, about whether or not there's a will."

He shrugged, smothered a yawn, then looked at the time. He was meeting a friend, a lawyer, in town at noon for drinks and lunch, and there were a number of other things he wanted to do first.

"Well, I must be off," he said, rising. "Mustn't keep the jolly old legal eagles waiting, must we? Not when I'm footing the bill for their time." He grinned cheerfully. "You could be looking at a man who's about to hear something to his advantage. That's if the home-made movie Queen Mae had on her when she snuffed it can be used in a court of law to prove she used witchcraft on my aunt to get her to change her will."

He paused, inclined his head contemplatively to one side. "You know, God's finally been good to me. I was beginning to wonder when my luck was going to change." He hesitated, thought for a moment. "Funny about that, though . . . Her being a witch. I should've thought that belonging to a coven would've required a fair sort of personal commitment, and I wouldn't have said Queen Mae had it in her. Ah well—" he grinned again "—who am I to look a gift horse in the mouth? Love to everyone back home," he said with a quick nod and another grin.

Mrs. Charles followed him out. He was at the bottom of the entrance steps by the time she crossed the porch.

The penguin waddled quickly away across the rain-puddled square, a furled black umbrella hooked jauntily in the crook of his right arm. He looked well pleased with himself. Indeed, as if he were someone, as he himself had said only a few minutes earlier, who was about to hear something to his advantage.

CHAPTER 11

An hour later, shortly before midday, Mrs. Charles unlatched the fancy, faded blue wrought-iron gate of No. 39 Wells Road, a pretty two-bedroomed red-brick and tile bungalow not dissimilar to her own, and then walked up a rose-bordered, crazy-paved path to the front door.

She had got the address from the telephone directory after having culled Mrs. Vera Markham's name from the morning paper. Vera Markham was described as being a widow with one son, and there was only one Mrs. V. Markham listed in the Gidding directory. The clairvoyante felt reasonably confident that she was calling on the right party.

Vera Markham was a while answering the doorbell. She was in the middle of making pastry for an apple tart, and when she eventually came to the door, she had a fluffy daub of flour on her chin and a dusting of it down the front of her green belted knit jacket. She was in her early fifties, wore no make-up over a flawless complexion, and had short, grey-streaked brown hair. Her brown eyes were lively, good-humoured.

"Mrs. Markham?" the clairvoyante inquired, and the other woman nodded and said, "Yes."

"I apologise for not telephoning," the clairvoyante then went on, "but I had to make a trip into Gidding this morning, and I decided that if I had some spare time, I would try and call and see you. My name is Edwina Charles. Mae Holliday was one of my clients. I was advising her on a problem of a deeply personal nature. She had an appointment with me on Wednesday—the day before she was murdered—and she was to have seen me again the following day."

"Oh," said Mrs. Markham. She wiped her floury hands on

the pink gingham apron tied round her waist and wondered (as the clairvoyante had hoped she would) about the nature of the "deeply personal problem" her caller had mentioned and whether she was to be made privy to it.

"I can see I've caught you at an awkward moment," said the clairvoyante, "but I wonder if you could possibly spare me a few minutes of your time? I read about you in this morning's paper, and it seemed to me that you were possibly the person most likely to be able to help me to clear up one or two queries I have concerning my client."

Her curiosity aroused and sure now that this smartly dressed, well-spoken woman (Mae Holliday's solicitor?—no, probably a doctor of one kind or another) was about to divulge some shattering revelation relating to the woman whose body she had discovered in Gidding Cathedral's Lady Chapel two days earlier, Mrs. Markham stepped back from the door and said, "Yes, of course. Come in, by all means. You don't mind if we talk in the kitchen, do you? I'm in the middle of making lunch for my elderly mother. She lives in the next street, and I slip round there most days with something special for her. She's marvellous, really," she said over her shoulder as Mrs. Charles followed her down the short hall. "Eighty-two and she still does most of her own shopping and cooking and all the cleaning."

They went into a modern, well-equipped kitchen.

"Please sit down," said Mrs. Markham, indicating a Windsor chair near the door to the garden. "That's Gran's—my mother's —favourite chair, but she won't mind—" She smiled. "She likes it for her back."

Mrs. Markham returned to the pine kitchen-table and began to knead the mound of dough waiting on the lightly floured board before her.

"It's strange how selfish people can be when they've got a problem weighing them down," she continued. "I remember feeling quite put out that someone—your client—was spending so much time in the Lady Chapel when I was waiting to use it. Oddly enough, it never once occurred to me that she was there probably for the same reason I was, because she was upset and worried about something. All I could think about was me, myself, and what a dreadful nuisance it was that I was being kept hanging about waiting on such a hot day. And all the while the poor woman was . . ."

Mrs. Markham sighed, shook her head and pounded the pastry again. Then she picked up a wooden rolling-pin, turned it on end and leaned on it for a moment or two. "As a matter of fact, I was only thinking about it as you rang the doorbell. The police took it quite amiss that I fell asleep while I was waiting to use the Lady Chapel and couldn't really tell them anything. But when you think about it, I was jolly lucky, wasn't I? That I slept through it all. When you think of what that monster did to her—your client—well, he wouldn't have thought twice about killing me too, would he? I mean, if I'd seen him going into the Lady Chapel and then coming out of it later, after he'd killed her. The police kept on and on at me, trying to get me to tell them something, and I couldn't because there wasn't anything I *could* tell them. I simply didn't see a thing."

"Sometimes," said the clairvoyante quietly, "a skilled interrogator can help a witness to recall things he or she might have observed without realising it."

Mrs. Markham, who was rolling out the pastry, paused and glanced up. "Putting words in your mouth, I call it," she said bluntly. She continued to roll out the pastry. "Well, I don't know about other people, but when *I* sleep it's with my eyes closed."

"It said in the paper, though, that you saw my client go into the Lady Chapel."

"Yes. I just caught a glimpse of her skirt. Then I saw her hand as she drew the curtain over the Lady Chapel."

"She was alone?"

"Yes. We—your client and I—were the only two people in the cathedral as far as I was concerned. I told all this to the police." Mrs. Markham looked at Mrs. Charles, puzzled. If this woman were a solicitor, or some kind of doctor, the police would surely have had no objection to giving her this information. . . .

Mrs. Charles saw the doubt begin to creep into the other woman's eyes and quickly took steps to assuage her fears. "Yes, of course. . . . I'm sorry, perhaps I should've been a little more specific. What I should've asked was, could you see into the Lady Chapel before my client drew the curtain?"

"Yes. The police asked me that too. It was empty. I got a clear view of the Lady Chapel as I walked across the back of the cathedral. I could see the altar and all the pews. The Lady Chapel isn't very big, you know, and the curtain was drawn by your client from the altar end of the chapel towards the back of the cathedral. From where I was standing up at the back, I could look straight into it. It was only the woman—your client —that I didn't see properly. Because of the curtain, which sort of shrouded her from view. I didn't get a good look at her until later. And my word, didn't it give me a nasty shock . . . seeing her lying there before the altar with that horrible *thing* sticking out of her. I fainted. Not right away, but when I got out to the street. I've never fainted before. Not even when the police came round here and told me about my—" She broke off, frowned slightly, lifted the rolled-out pastry on to a glass dish, and then deftly trimmed it to size with a sharp knife. "But that's not got anything to do with your client," she sighed. "What was it that you wanted to know?"

"Would you mind telling me exactly what you did after you'd seen my client draw the curtain over the Lady Chapel?"

Mrs. Markham raised her eyebrows a little at the question but complied.

"I walked down the aisle and then—"

"The centre aisle or the one at the side of the Lady Chapel?"

"That one. I walked slowly past the Lady Chapel, then I sat down on one of the pews in the cathedral, and the next thing I knew it was one-fifteen. I suddenly looked at the time and realised I'd been asleep for over half an hour. So I gathered my things together and started to leave, but as I was walking back up the aisle, my shopping bags got caught up in the curtain over the Lady Chapel and I dragged it along with me. It hangs on large wooden curtain-rings and moves fairly freely both ways, to the right or the left. I didn't like to leave it like that, partly open, so I put my things down and . . . Well, that was when I glanced into the Lady Chapel and saw her, your client."

"You slept soundly for that half-hour? You didn't keep waking up and dozing off again?"

Mrs. Markham shook her head as she spooned cold stewed apples from a small saucepan over the pastry in the dish. "No. As you know, it was very hot that day, and I'd been shopping all morning. I was absolutely exhausted." She put the saucepan aside and glanced up at Mrs. Charles. "I'm awfully sorry I can't be more helpful, but like I told the police, I went out like a light. I didn't see or hear a thing other than what I've already told you. I was too busy worrying about what St. Anthony was going to tell my mother the next time she prayed to him."

She laughed self-consciously, picked up the sharp knife, and began to cut a series of thin strips of pastry. "You'd never believe the silly dream I had about him and my mother while I was asleep in the cathedral. He was some sort of judge, I think. You know what dreams are like," she said as she artistically criss-crossed the tart with the strips of pastry. "Nothing's terribly clear—my dreams aren't, anyway. I've always got to guess who this person or that person is and what they're saying and doing. Then when I wake up I spend hours trying to work out what it's all supposed to mean."

She paused and turned her head reflectively on one side. Then, shrugging: "I can't for the life of me think what it could've been that I had on me that day which would get my lad Brian into trouble if St. Anthony found out about it. It's really preyed on my mind, you know. I feel so guilty about it all the time. There wasn't any mention of it in the papers this morning—the court case is *sub judice,* or whatever it is they say when no one's supposed to talk about it—but my lad's been in a spot of bother with the police, got himself mixed up in some bad company down in London, and I woke up from my dream just as St. Anthony was going to pass judgment on him —or me—I'm not sure now which it was—and I could tell it was going to be bad news. It was the way St. Anthony used that little hammer of his to bring the court to attention . . . sort of apologetically, when I came to think about it. As if he was sorry to wake me up when all he had for me was bad news. Some people knock on your door like that when all they want from you is an answer to some silly question or other and they're a bit embarrassed about disturbing you. And that was when I came to . . . or soon afterwards. So I never got to hear what St. Anthony had to say to me. But that's the way of dreams, isn't it? Leaving you hanging up in mid-air like that."

"Was there any sound with your dream?" asked the clairvoyante.

"Yes, a little. At least, I think so. You know how it is. As time passes, the dream begins to fade and you're no longer sure about anything."

"How loud would you say this sound was?" the clairvoyante persisted.

"Was it loud enough to be real? you mean," said Mrs. Markham matter-of-factly. She hesitated, frowned. "I thought about that myself afterwards. My dreams don't usually come with a full stereophonic sound-track—" she smiled "—and I wondered if the hammering noise I'd heard could've been one of the men working in the cloisters on the north wall of the cathedral—round the other side of the Lady Chapel—but my mother said the workmen took down all their scaffolding and finished up there at the end of last week."

"Was there anybody else working on the cathedral that day?"

"Mother says not. A friend of hers was telling her that there won't be any more work done on the cathedral now until they've raised more money. The restoration of the cloisters cleaned them out. It was one of those jobs that cost more and more the farther the work progressed. Once they actually got down to business, the amount of work needed to be done was far greater than anyone had realised. And that reminds me," said Mrs. Markham with a quick frown. "I must remember to look out those odd bits of knitting-wool for Mother and take them round with me today. She's crocheting a wool blanket to help raise money for the restoration fund. It's going to be raffled at the summer bazaar. One of the church deacons called round specially to thank her. Not that Mother answered the door to him. Against her principles," she laughed. "The daft thing hid behind the curtain in the hall when she saw who was knocking on her door. But she was tickled pink about it all the same when Mrs. Frearson—one of her friends—told her why the deacon had called. Mother likes to think she's an atheist," Mrs. Markham explained. Then, with a smile: "She'd have been a hippie if they'd had them when she was a girl."

"Frearson," said the clairvoyante meditatively. "Wasn't there some mention of someone with that name in the paper this morning?"

Mrs. Markham nodded. "The lace-edged handkerchief the police found with your client's things . . . it was one of Mrs. Frearson's, the lady I was just talking about—my mother's friend. She made it. Only the newspaper reports got it all wrong about the forget-me-nots. Mrs. Frearson never did any of that sort of embroidery work on her lace handkerchiefs."

"This Mrs. Frearson is in some way connected with the Lady Chapel, is she?"

"No, not specifically with the Lady Chapel. Before she went blind, she used to make all the altar cloths for the altar in the cathedral as well as the one in the Lady Chapel. The lacework on the handkerchiefs she made always featured the heraldic emblem, a white iris—the fleur-de-lis—of the Bourne family . . . the aristocrats who built the Lady Chapel. The fleur-de-lis was always worked into the lace for the altar cloths for the Lady Chapel too. The handkerchiefs were sold to visitors to the cathedral to raise money for the restoration fund."

"Perhaps the police made a mistake and my client's lace handkerchief wasn't one of those made by Mrs. Frearson."

"Oh, I don't think the police would be likely to make that sort of mistake. Not about one of Mrs. Frearson's handkerchiefs. She's famous for them in Gidding. The fleur-de-lis in her lacework makes it quite unique, very distinctive and easy to identify. No, any mistake that's been made has been the newspaper reporter's. The fleur-de-lis was Mrs. Frearson's trademark. She must've made hundreds of those lace hankies in her time. It's such a shame to see her now; in perfect health, but unable to do any more fine needlework. A little crocheting and some knitting is about the most she can manage these days. My mother visits her once a week and they sit and crochet together, keep each other company. They've been friends for years. Ever since their school-days."

Mrs. Markham turned aside to put the tart in the oven. "You're not from around here, Gidding, are you?" she said.

"No. I live on the outskirts of the village of Little Gidding."

Mrs. Markham nodded. "I guessed as much—that you were a stranger—when you didn't know about Mrs. Frearson. She used to be quite a celebrity in her younger days. There was always somebody wanting to interview her about her lacework. She brought a lot of visitors to the town."

"Was her lacework on sale anywhere else, in any of the shops in town?"

"Good heavens, no. She couldn't have kept up with the demand. She was approached once by some linen manufacturer who makes handkerchiefs—he wanted permission to turn them out by the thousand—but nothing ever came of it. A pity in a way, but then again it wouldn't have been quite the same, would it? Being able to buy one of the Lady Chapel fleur-de-lis lace handkerchiefs from just any old shop in town."

"You could only buy them at the cathedral?"

Mrs. Markham started to clear up. "Yes. There used to be a little stall of booklets for sale to the left of the main doorway of the cathedral. I can't say I noticed it while I was there on Thursday, but it's probably still somewhere around. You used to be able to buy the handkerchiefs there, and occasionally at some of the cathedral's fund-raising events. I used to have one myself years ago. Mrs. Frearson made one specially for me for my birthday one year. I could kick myself now that I didn't hang on to it. I was much too young to appreciate it—I was only thirteen. It was just another handkerchief to me then. I think I lost it in the finish."

The delicious smell of the tart baking in the oven began to fill the kitchen.

Mrs. Charles rose.

"I wish I could've been more helpful," said Mrs. Markham, wiping her hands on a cloth.

Moving out into the hall, Mrs. Charles paused and said, "I don't suppose it's possible that the hammering noise in your dream was actually someone's footsteps echoing in the cathedral?"

"No, it was nothing like that sort of sound," said Mrs. Markham without hesitation. "It could've been someone knocking on a door to be let in, but the cathedral doors are always wide open, aren't they? They were that day, anyhow."

"Yes," said Mrs. Charles slowly. "They were wide open this morning when I called there."

Mrs. Markham hesitated. Then: "I hope you don't think me rude for asking you this, but you said Miss Holliday was your client. You were her solicitor, were you?"

"No, Mrs. Markham," said Mrs. Charles. "Her clairvoyante."

"Clairvoyante!"

Dumbfounded, Mrs. Markham closed the door and gazed through the pebble-glass at the blurred figure walking away from her. "You've been conned, Vera Markham, my girl," she said to herself out loud. "Conned good and proper. Sucked right in. Serves you right for being such a Nosey Parker!"

With a startled exclamation, she suddenly remembered the tart and dashed back to the kitchen to rescue it. Another minute and she would have been too late.

She set the dish on a stand to cool, paused and frowned. Her thoughts went back over what she had read that morning about the home-made movie found in Mae Holliday's skirt-pocket, and she began to feel uneasy.

What if that woman who had just called was one of them? A

member of—what was it they belonged to—a coven? What if she was a witch and she'd been sent round to check up on her and find out just how much she really knew?

Mrs. Markham sank into the Windsor chair, then quickly sprang upright and turned and stared at it fearfully, as if it had been cursed by some terrible spell that had now attached itself to her person.

"Oh, my God," she said aloud. "You silly bitch, Vera. What have you done?"

CHAPTER 12

The appointment Mrs. Charles had made with the superintendent of St. Anthony's Village was for two in the afternoon. He had said it was the quietest and therefore most convenient hour of day for him to see her, as most of the elderly ladies in his care took a short nap immediately after lunch and there were fewer demands on his time.

The superintendent's office, like the small bungalows attractively laid out in the garden village, was neat and compact. A framed print of Rudyard Kipling's *If* hung on the left-hand wall over a narrow shelf. There was a small clock on the shelf, an empty cut-glass flower vase, and a solitary cactus in a tiny black plastic pot. A shrimp plant stood on the window-ledge in the watery sunshine which washed intermittently over the window. The rain had eased off while Mrs. Charles was talking to Arthur Dunphie in Gidding Cathedral, and it hadn't rained heavily since, though it seemed likely that it would before long. The sky was steadily darkening and a wind was getting up.

The man who came round his desk to greet the clairvoyante —although David Sayer had forewarned her—was older than she had expected. His hair, which might once have been quite curly, was white and sparse, a low part on the left-hand side enabling him to comb long, fuzzy strands over his otherwise bald, freckled scalp. His face was long and thin, pitted with scars from smallpox, which he had contracted when working as a missionary in India, while a slight stroke several years ago had left him with a partial facial paralysis affecting his right eye, which most people assumed was merely "lazy." He was fifty-five but looked a good ten years older, possibly only temporarily through grief. He sounded tired when he spoke and looked generally exhausted.

Reading the clairvoyante's thoughts about his age, Jocelyn Smith smiled as they shook hands and said, "Yes, the police were a little surprised too . . . at the wide age gap between Mae and myself." He gestured to a chair and Mrs. Charles sat down. He looked at her for a moment, seemed lost in thought. Then, with a quick frown: "It bothered me quite a lot—this was when I realised that Mae and I were becoming . . . well, rather fond of one another—her being only thirty-two and me well into my fifties. I knew how I felt, what my intentions—motives—were, but I wasn't sure about her. It was a long time before I felt able to tell her what my feelings were. It worried me that in her eyes, I was little more than a surrogate father—I merely reminded her of someone she'd once been very close to."

"Her father, you mean?"

Jocelyn Smith sat down, shook his head sadly. "I don't know, I never found out. Mae never spoke about her family. She made it clear very early on in our friendship that it was an area of her life which she preferred not to discuss. So I left it right alone. I felt sure that when the time was right, she would confide in me. I fancy there was something rather unpleasant in her past that she was keeping locked up inside her. I wouldn't know, you understand, but in my line of work you get to be a fairly shrewd amateur psychologist, and my guess would be that she had a tough time of it when she was very young."

He frowned absently, then seemed to give himself a little shake. Leaning forward, he smiled tiredly and said, "Forgive me. You came to see me, and here I am not giving you a chance to get a word in edgewise. When you phoned this morning, you said Mae consulted you the day before she was murdered. . . ."

"You didn't seem terribly surprised," observed the clairvoyante.

He frowned again. "To be perfectly frank, you phoned in

the middle of a mini-crisis. One of our residents had slipped and fallen while stepping out of the bath-tub and broken a hip: I'd just seen her off in an ambulance and was on the point of contacting her son when you rang. I was really only half-listening to you. It wasn't until I'd rung off that it really hit me—what you'd said—and then I wasn't too sure that I'd got it straight." He eyed Mrs. Charles speculatively. "You said Mae came to you to have her fortune told?"

"No. I said I was a clairvoyante and that Miss Holliday had consulted me."

He looked stricken, as if she had struck him an unexpected blow to the face. "I hope not about us, Mae and me—our friendship. She wasn't having doubts, was she? Second thoughts? I'd hate to think I'd rushed things, though I admit that I was perhaps a little over-anxious to get things settled between us. I was going to ask her to marry me, you know, and perhaps she sensed it—women are pretty intuitive about these things—and she didn't feel quite ready. . . ."

"No, it had nothing to do with you, Mr. Smith. In fact, at that stage, I knew nothing of your friendship with her. Miss Holliday never referred to it."

He looked at her steadily. "I don't know quite how to take that, whether it's a good thing or a bad thing that Mae made no mention of me and our friendship."

"She would've only done that, Mr. Smith," said Mrs. Charles quietly, "if your relationship with her had been causing her some concern, which it obviously wasn't." Something of a white lie, the clairvoyante acknowledged to herself, but justifiable in the circumstances. There was no point now in telling Jocelyn Smith that she believed that Mae Holliday would never have married him had she been unable to discover her true origins.

"Naturally, I'm curious about why she came to see you," he said, "but I'll understand perfectly if you'd prefer not to discuss it with me."

"I can only tell you what you yourself already know, that

Miss Holliday had something locked tightly inside her that was deeply troubling her."

"And you won't tell me what that something was?"

"I don't know what it was . . . any more than you do. Neither did she."

The puzzled expression on his face deepened and the "lazy" appearance of his right eye seemed suddenly more pronounced. "Are you saying that Mae was suffering from some kind of psychological disturbance, a mental block?"

"Amnesia," she said simply.

"*Mae?*" He looked at her incredulously, then quickly shook his head. "No, forgive me if I'm being impolite, but that's not possible. I'm sure I would've spotted something of that nature. There'd have been more blanks in her life, periods she couldn't account for. No," he said again, more firmly this time. "I'd definitely have recognised the signs. While I admit she never once referred to her family background, she talked a lot about the past—people she'd known, things she'd done, places she'd been."

"Yes, but over what period of time? How far back into her past did she go?"

He hesitated, thought for a moment. "Well, now that you come to mention it, she only ever talked about the village—Little Gidding—the years she'd spent there."

"She never mentioned Gidding to you—the town of Gidding?"

"No. That came as a complete surprise to me when the police told me that their investigations had given them to believe that she was a Gidding girl. I don't know why, but my impression was that she originally came from much further afield. From somewhere up North would've been my guess. But I don't know, it is only a guess. And to be honest with you, I never gave it a moment's thought until I found out from the police about her having come from Gidding. It was then I suddenly realised that subconsciously I'd somehow accepted that she was from the North—Lancashire, or possibly Yorkshire."

"Did she ever refer to her connection with Gidding Cathedral—St. Anthony's?"

He shook his head. "No. That was another shock. I'd never been able to get Mae anywhere near a church, and yet there she was in the cathedral's Lady Chapel, of all places. I wouldn't go so far as to say she was an agnostic, but she was definitely very anti-Church. Anti anything to do with organised religion."

"Wouldn't that have made things a little awkward for you?"

"With this job, my superintendency here, you mean?" He was quiet for a moment. "I hoped not. I always felt that whatever it was that had gone wrong in Mae's life was somehow linked with the Church, or with religion generally. In some ways, she reminded me of a small boy I once knew who became seriously psychologically disturbed after seeing a crucifix in a church for the first time, and thereafter screamed in terror every time his mother attempted to take him into a church. But, as I've said, I hoped that in time, she would turn to me and confide in me and that we'd have been able to face the problem together. Regardless of what it was."

"Including a confession that she was a practising witch?"

He looked at the clairvoyante thoughtfully, wondered if she were trying to tell him something . . . that there was a witches' coven meeting secretly in the village and that both she and Mae were members of it? (Maybe there was some secret sign like the Freemasons used, and she was checking to see if he was familiar with it and therefore knew that Mae had been mixed up in occult practices.) There was another avenue of thought too that ought to be explored, the possibility that this woman sitting before him was mentally deranged, a crackpot. She didn't look mad, but then insanity came in many different guises. And the police had warned him that one of the more unfortunate aspects of this kind of murder investigation was the large number of cranks it attracted, and that he should be on the alert for them, they might possibly seek him out.

"If it had come down to it," he said at length. "Yes, even

that. I don't know how Mae got hold of that home-made movie the police discovered in her possession. I'm quite sure it didn't belong to her." He looked distressed, his face greyed. "The police ran it through for me: they hoped I'd be able to help them to establish whether or not it was a movie of Mae when she was a child."

A shiny dew-drop of moisture had formed in the corner of his bad eye, which made him look even more distressed. "I must say it was a most unpleasant experience. Quite horrid. Morbid. Sick. I told them—this was when they asked me if I'd mind taking a look at it for them—that they were wasting their time, I'd never seen any pictures of Mae as a little girl. I'm hopeless at picking likenesses, anyway. Especially in females. Women change so. Different hair-styles, hair colouring . . . And it's amazing how a woman can change her facial appearance with cosmetics—all this weird eye-shadow and shiny stuff they smear on their cheeks and lips these days. Mae, I know, never wore make-up, but she still looked nothing like the child in the film to me. Besides, the little girl appeared to have your colouring, blonde hair and a very fair complexion. Mae's hair was brown."

"My brother has Miss Holliday's colouring, dark eyes and mid-brown hair, but as a child he had long golden-blond ringlets."

"It still didn't look like Mae to me," he said with a slow shake of his head. "Nothing like her at all. Though I admit the film was of very poor quality."

He paused, thought for a moment or two. "I couldn't quite see the point of it all . . . why the police were so interested in the film and who was in it when they knew who'd killed Mae. Still, I daresay they've got to look into that sort of thing, especially when a child's involved. That's if one believes what one reads in some of the Sunday papers and there really is a growing interest in Satanism, and children—babies, I read only last week—are being used as sacrifices. I've never taken any of it too seriously myself."

He looked at the clairvoyante and seemed, she thought, to

be waiting for her to confirm or deny what he had just said. Or
was he another one, like Arthur Dunphie, she wondered whim-
sically, who was looking for some physical evidence that she
was a witch—like pointed ears, or the more traditional hooked
nose and warts?

After a moment, he said softly, "No, I'm sure I would've
known if Mae were a witch. We hadn't known one another
long, I admit that, but surely there would've been signs . . . ?"

He looked at the clairvoyante but again failed to draw any
reaction from her, though he began to feel even more certain
that she was testing him in some way to see if he would let
anything slip about Mae. He went on, sighing deeply: "Mae
was a deeply troubled, intensely unhappy woman. She used to
laugh at me for the way I looked at life—my work here with
the elderly, and how I saw it as my mission in life. She didn't
realise," he said gravely, "that this was how I felt about her
too. I loved her—don't misunderstand me there—but she was
another mission, another goal I'd set myself and had high
hopes of accomplishing. I had the patience; all I needed was a
little time."

"The superintendent's post attached to this type of estab-
lishment is usually shared by a married couple, isn't it? Was it
your intention that Miss Holliday should join you in your work
here?"

He smiled fleetingly. "'Tell me thy reason why thou wilt
marry.'"

He paused, smiled again. "'My poor body, madam, requires
it: I am driven on by the flesh. . . .'" His smile saddened.
"You put that—your doubts about Mae as a suitable candidate
for a job working intimately with elderly folk—very nicely." He
raised an eyebrow at her. "That was, I think, what you really
meant." He wiped a hand across his eyes, then nodded tiredly.
"Yes, I know Mae found it difficult to get along with people,
and maybe it was foolish of me to think it could ever have
been otherwise. I freely admit that I was anxious to remarry
partly because of my work here. I was under no pressure from
the Church, but I knew everyone would feel much happier if I

had a woman, a wife, working at my side as my late wife Olive had; and I was optimistic that once Mae had embarked upon the stable relationship that marriage provides—or should provide—she'd feel more relaxed and secure and be less hostile and aggressive. In the words of St. Francis—" he smiled again sadly "—she would not so much seek to be understood, as to understand. She was terribly insecure, you know." He was quiet for a moment.

Then: "She was so different, the complete opposite of Olive. My wife died unexpectedly of a heart attack the year after I took up my post here as superintendent. It was a very bitter blow. We'd just begun to relax and settle down properly into the work here after going through an extremely bad patch. I was made redundant after many years' service with an old, established engineering company here in Gidding, which, like everywhere else right now, has a high unemployment problem extending back over the past five years; and then just when it seemed that I'd never get another job—because of my age and health problems (I suffered a minor stroke not long after I'd been made redundant)—I heard about this post here at St. Anthony's Village and decided to try for it. We—Olive and I—couldn't believe our good fortune when I landed it. We were very happy together here. The job was—and still is—everything we could've wished for. And then the unthinkable happened, Olive died—two years ago next Saturday, as a matter of fact—and I just couldn't believe it; any more than I can believe this, that Mae too is gone. I have always accepted what I believe to be a simple truth—there are no errors in God's great eternal plan. Every misfortune, no matter how terrible, has its purpose, and while we might not be able to see or understand it at the time, all things work in harmony for the ultimate good of mankind.

"And even though these are difficult days for me, I know that in some way it is a test of my faith, and that in time, and with hindsight, I will look back and be able to say—"

The telephone rang shrilly, and he excused himself, picked

up the receiver, spoke for a few moments, made some notes on a pad, and then rang off.

"The hospital," he explained. "Mrs. Franklin—the lady who had the fall in the bath-tub this morning . . . the staff nurse wants me to get some of her things ready for her son to pick up."

"I won't keep you," said Mrs. Charles, rising. She hesitated. "There was just one other thing, and I hope you won't think me impertinent for asking it. Was it somewhere here in Gidding that you and Miss Holliday first met?"

"No, it was in the village, Little Gidding." He cast his mind back. "About eighteen months ago . . . when I called into the post office for directions. One of our residents had died, and I went over to the village to offer my condolences to the deceased's family. As you know, most of the roads and lanes in the village don't have names. Or if they do, it has to be one of the best kept secrets of all time—" He smiled. "And what with half the houses being neither named nor numbered, I was well and truly lost. I'd still be over there searching for the right party if it hadn't been for Mae setting me straight."

"I have a new newspaper delivery boy who's currently in similar difficulties," said Mrs. Charles with a smile.

"I don't know how strangers find their way around the place. Mae—and Mrs. Cockburn—must've got fed up with giving people directions. . . ."

"We don't get many visitors," said the clairvoyante.

"I'm not surprised," he said.

CHAPTER 13

David was in two minds as to whom he should call on first, the clairvoyante or John Little, better known in the village as Little John, Big John Little's eighty-five-year-old father.

A heavy thunderstorm made the decision for him. David disliked driving on the motorway in teeming rain and with thunder and lightning flashing about him; and at three-thirty when he set out for the village, with more stormy black clouds building up in the north, he opted for the secondary roads and narrow lanes, the long way round. This meant he would now have to drive straight through the heart of Little Gidding, past John Little's cottage, to reach the clairvoyante's semi-isolated bungalow, which was on the motorway side of the village.

It had stopped raining and the storm-clouds were beginning to disperse again by the time David reached the old man's ramshackle cottage on the outskirts of the village. Like the bungalow, it too was semi-isolated, the Littles' nearest neighbours being a quarter of a mile away in the village itself.

David could see Little John from the road. The old man was in the weed-overrun back garden boiling withies in a brick, coal-fired willow boiler. No one now could recall who had dubbed John Little "Little John," but anyone could see why. Little John was as spare, frail and fragile-looking as his fifty-five-year-old son was big, hail and hearty.

Little John saw the ex-police officer approaching him, but he made no sign to this effect and went on with his work. He knew David, had known him since David was a small boy. He also knew why he had come.

David joined him at the steaming boiler, glanced up at the blue-patched sky.

"We've had a drop or two today, Little John," said David by way of greeting.

"Aye," said the old man without pausing at his work. "It be damp right enough."

"Gets in your bones," said David.

"Aye."

The old man went on working. He would be there for some hours. Big John had been busy. There was a great stack of withies waiting for a turn in the boiler. A short distance from the boiler was the big wooden frame Big John used to weave the boiled withies into hurdles for fences.

"They've not found that lad of yours yet," said David.

"Oh aye," said the old man. Then, after a slight pause: "Didn't really expect they would."

"You know where he is, don't you?" guessed David.

"Aye," the old man admitted. "Came home when it looked like rain, didn't he?"

"He's here now?"

"Aye. In withy shed." The old man inclined his head over his shoulder. "Been there all night."

David looked at the crumbling stone and slate shed at the bottom of the garden. The broken wooden door was half open, and he assumed that Big John was busy inside stacking the withies from the boiler.

"D'you mind if I have a word with him?"

"Suit yerself. He told me them witnesses what saw him outside church in Gidding got it all wrong. He was on his way t'pub to wet his whistle. Same as always."

David nodded sympathetically, then when the old man had nothing further to say, he slowly drifted away. He approached the withy shed cautiously. As a rule, Big John did most of his heavy drinking down at the Black Swan late at night, so David did not expect him to be in an advanced state of drunken belligerency at the present moment. He hoped he would be approachable, drunk or sober. He wasn't sure what to expect.

He stood for a moment outside the door listening to the unnerving stillness within. There were no windows in the shed, and its interior, with the exception of a narrow shaft of sepia-tinted light from the doorway, was dark and murky. He waited for his eyes to adjust to the gloom, but he could still barely see a thing in there.

David glanced back at the old man, who took no notice of him and continued with his work.

"Big John?" David called out loudly.

He waited for a while, listened intently. Nothing. Complete silence. Then, edgily: "I know you're in there, Big John."

David put a hand on the door, gave it a gentle, tentative push. It opened stiffly, groaned a little, dropped an inch or two on its sagging hinges.

Something made him look up.

Small scraps of pale blue sky showed through the roof where here and there a slate tile was missing.

A pair of big-booted feet dangled in mid-air.

Big John was hanging by his neck from one of the heavy beamed rafters.

David was not his usual apologetic self. He was displeased about something—with her, the clairvoyante suspected—and upset. Very upset. He didn't say why, not immediately. He didn't need to. He had come, as she had known he would, to tell her about Big John, that he had quit the alder marshes and was dead.

She had found David waiting for her in his car outside her bungalow when she had returned from Gidding shortly before five o'clock that evening after seeing Jocelyn Smith.

David followed her indoors without saying a word.

"Well, Superintendent?" The clairvoyante finished pouring the straight whisky he generally preferred, looked up at him contemplatively.

"I have always respected your confidence, Madame," he said as she handed him his drink. "At times at the expense of the privileged relationship I enjoy—and would wish to continue to enjoy—with the senior police officers stationed at Gidding Constabulary. In return I would not have deemed it unreasonable of me to expect that you would do nothing to jeopardise that special relationship. Certainly not without first consulting with me."

She looked at him thoughtfully. "Yes, Superintendent?" she said when he did not continue.

A flash of annoyance illuminated his face. "Really, Madame! You go over to Gidding, scare the life out of Vera Markham. . . . Have you any idea how I felt when Clive Merton contacted me about your visit—because he knows that you and I are personal friends—and wanted to know what the hell was going on, and I had to admit I knew that Mae Holliday was a client of yours and had actually consulted you the day before she was murdered?"

The clairvoyante's eyebrows rose. "Mrs. Markham contacted the police about my visit to her this morning?"

"Screaming blue murder! She thinks you're a witch!"

"Oh dear," said the clairvoyante with a small smile.

"It's not funny, Madame," he said coldly.

"No, perhaps not." She looked at him. "I can't be held responsible for the strange things people think, Superintendent."

"What's so strange about it?" he asked heatedly. "The newspapers as good as say Mae Holliday was mixed up in devil worship, witchcraft, and then you turn up on her front doorstep asking all sorts of weird and wonderful questions. The poor woman is terrified that you called for the express purpose of putting a hex on her and her family."

"That, Superintendent, is what comes of being honest with people," said Mrs. Charles pleasantly. "I can see I'm going to have to try and be a lot more devious in future."

"I doubt that it'll require much effort," he snapped.

She smiled. Then, after a brief pause: "So Mrs. Markham telephoned the police. . . ." She was quiet for a moment. "She didn't seem the hysterical type."

"She wasn't exactly hysterical, Madame. But she was scared."

"Of me? How silly."

He frowned at her. "No, not silly. Sensible. She did the right thing. Merton thinks so and I agree with him." His eyes narrowed. "Especially if Mae Holliday was a practising witch and there is a coven somewhere in the village."

"Ah, we're back to that again, are we?" sighed the clairvoyante.

"I asked you right at the beginning to go to the police," he said crossly. "You've met Merton: he's not a bad sort of chap. You could've at least *talked* to him." His eyes widened. "You realise, don't you, that things can never be the same between myself and the lads over at Gidding because of this? You've let me down badly, Madame. You knew Mae Holliday was involved in black magic. You should've told the police that, and you certainly owed it to me to tell me."

"But I didn't know that Mae Holliday was a witch, Superintendent," said the clairvoyante calmly. "I still don't know it. Though since speaking to you last, I now think it's a possibility —not necessarily that she was a witch, but that she was involved at some time in her life with people who practised black magic."

"Here in the village?" he asked quickly.

The clairvoyante hesitated. "I'm not sure. It depends. First and foremost on whether or not Mae Holliday was the child in that home-made movie."

"Merton is still of the opinion that it is, or was, her."

"But he's not sure."

"No. He's been trying to trace her relatives in the hope that someone will be able to identify her—the child in the movie, that is—but she doesn't appear to have had any family at all. Her boy-friend, Jocelyn Smith, said he couldn't remember her ever having referred to anyone, and Tilly Cockburn from the store says the same thing. The same goes for Arthur Dunphie, Agatha's nephew. She was all alone in the world as far as all three of them were concerned."

David paused, frowned. "If there are people, adults, in the village who want to go down to the woods at night to shed their clothes and play ring-a-rosy in the moonlight, there's not all that much anybody can do about it. But if children from the village are involved and are being used in some kind of pagan sacrificial ceremony, real or make-believe, then that's another matter. It's got to be investigated, Madame. Mae Holliday went into that church in Gidding on Thursday for some specific reason connected with that reel of movie-film. The police think so, I think so. If the Lady Chapel was, and is, being used by Mae Holliday and others for purposes other than those for which it was properly intended, then the police and the Church want to know, so they can stamp it right out before the disease spreads. I understand that the Church would've preferred that no mention be made of the content of the film, and that it's now considering closing the Lady Chapel to the public for a cooling-off period. St. Anthony's desperately needs visitors—tourists—but of the right sort, Madame. I believe there's a meeting tonight to decide what to do about the matter. It's a very regrettable situation from the Church's point of view. The Lady Chapel is one of St. Anthony's principal tourist attractions, with an unblemished history, and in one fell swoop, Mae Holliday and her coven—if there is one—have wiped all that out completely, possibly forever. Now when sightseers visit the Lady Chapel, you can bet it won't be the Bourne family they're interested in.

"The Church is most concerned—and with good reason, I'd say," he went on, "that the publicity over that reel of movie-film will attract other Satanists to the Lady Chapel like flies to the honey-pot. All sorts of weirdos and crackpots. Though I would imagine that any local coven—including the one it seems likely Mae Holliday belonged to, which might've been using the Lady Chapel for its Black Masses or whatever—will steer clear of it until all the publicity has died down."

"Have the police any idea yet where the movie was made?"

"No. It could've been shot just about anywhere—in Gidding or even here in the village."

"But Mae Holliday didn't live in the village twenty years ago when you said the movie was made," the clairvoyante reminded him.

"No, and maybe there wasn't a coven here then, either."

"She brought one with her when she moved to the village?"

"Or the coven followed her. They don't like defections from their ranks, do they?"

The clairvoyante hesitated. Then she said thoughtfully, "The police have changed their minds about Big John, have they?"

"No, Madame. It was just bad luck—one of those bizarre quirks of fate—that it happened to be market-day and Big John saw her going into the cathedral and followed her. The two are not linked; it's 'case closed' as far as the murder investigation is concerned—as of approximately four-fifteen this afternoon."

"The police found Big John?" Over and above the sadness and regret in Mrs. Charles's voice was her quiet acceptance of the inevitability of the prophecy of the Tarot for Big John once he left the sanctuary of the alder marshes.

"No, I did—in his withy shed. He was dead. Hanged by the neck. He'd used the leather belt from his trousers, kicked a chair out from under his feet."

David was too personally distressed to notice and therefore wonder at the clairvoyante's calm reaction to the news. He went on, "His old dad found him dead early this morning. Incredibly stoic about it."

Shaking his head, David paused and pictured the old man calmly boiling withies as if it were just another ordinary day. "All he said was, 'Her in post office drove him to it.'"

"To commit suicide or to kill Mae Holliday?"

"I thought he meant both." David looked at her keenly. "You've had second thoughts about Big John, haven't you?"

The clairvoyante hesitated before replying, chose her words carefully. "I had no reason yesterday when you called to think it might've been someone other than him who had killed her, and his father's comment on his suicide would seem an end to the matter."

"But why go and see Vera Markham?"

"To find out the truth. To get answers to questions which have no answers."

"I don't understand, Madame," he said slowly.

"No, Superintendent. Neither do I. But when I do, you will be the first to know."

CHAPTER 14

It was time, Mrs. Charles decided, that she and her brother had a talk.

She fetched her suede jacket—it had turned quite cool in the past hour—and a headscarf in case it started to rain again, and went out. David had left twenty minutes earlier saying that he intended to call in at his aunt's. Miss Sayer was entertaining her friend, Helena Winfield from St. Anthony's Village, to tea, and David had been seconded to drive her guest home afterwards.

Mrs. Charles looked back along the road towards Miss Sayer's cottage. David's car was still there. Nearer, Mr. Curry was in his greenhouse. He was bending over looking at something, probably tending some potted plants—it was a little too far away for Mrs. Charles to see exactly what he was doing. She would need binoculars for that, she thought with a small smile.

She kept well on to the grassy verge. Her brother's house, one part of a large farm before the motorway was built, was the last of the six properties situated in the road before one reached the slip-road giving access to the motorway.

The tall wireless aerials in Cyril Forbes's long front garden—some of the trappings of his space-monitoring programme—swayed in a stiff breeze. Mrs. Charles glanced at them as she passed and hoped Cyril would not be "On the Air." It was a little early yet, nowhere near dark enough, for him to be up in the loft looking at the heavens through the powerful telescope he kept housed up there. But this was where he would be later, where he would probably spend most of the night.

He was in the study writing an article for his space maga-

zine. His black, yellow-eyed cat, James, was curled up alongside him on the worn leather chesterfield. Mrs. Charles wasn't
too sure whether her brother had acquired the cat, or the cat
had acquired Cyril. The latter, she suspected. Since taking up
residence with Cyril, James had earned the reputation of being
the meanest-tempered cat in the village. No tradesman would
call at the house, and even the postman now waited in his van
out in the road for Cyril to come and collect his mail from him.
(This was after James "got" Alf Turner, the postman—savagely
mauled his hand—through the mail-slot.) But James was very
tolerant with Mrs. Charles. He seemed to know she was "family," but he was never completely at ease when she was there
and came as close as a cat could to smiling when she would
finally get up and leave.

James sat up when she came into the room and watched her
thoughtfully as she cleared a pile of dusty magazines from a
chair before sitting down on it. Cyril simply went on writing.

"Do you think I could interrupt you for just a moment,
Cyril?" Mrs. Charles asked after a long moment's silence
showed every promise of stretching into an eternity.

It was a minute or more before he responded, then he
glanced up, nodded, went on writing.

"I wanted to ask you something about the Lady Chapel in
St. Anthony's."

Her brother made no comment.

"Are you listening to me, Cyril?"

He looked up. "I'm listening." He continued writing.

"Was the Lady Chapel ever associated in any way with talk
of witchcraft while you were singing in the church choir?"
Mrs. Charles paused. Then: "Was there, for example, ever any
evidence, anything at all to suggest that a Black Mass might've
been celebrated there?"

There was another long silence.

"Cyril?" said Mrs. Charles at length.

He glanced up at her. "Go on," he said. "I'm listening."

She gave up. "I'll make an appointment with James," she

said, getting to her feet, "and call round some other time when it's more convenient for you to talk."

"Yes," he said, still writing. "He's your man. He'll sort things out for you."

James dropped gracefully on to the floor and politely saw Mrs. Charles to the front door. She could almost hear his sigh of relief as she closed it behind her.

As she reached the road, David drove past with Helena Winfield—a shrivelled, round-shouldered woman of seventy-one with a hard, wrinkled face and no hair that was visible under a tight-fitting, pleated white turban other than for a two-inch wide steel-grey bang which lay flat and straight across her brow high above a long, sharp nose. Helena Winfield was talking animatedly, and with some relish, about what the surgeons had found inside Mrs. So-and-So's (nobody David knew) stomach when they had opened her up. His aunt, thought David wryly, as he gave Mrs. Charles a quick wave, must be unique amongst Helena Winfield's friends and acquaintances, the only one who hadn't undergone major abdominal surgery, who wasn't lying at death's door or hadn't actually passed through it!

"Your aunt's taking poor Mrs. Franklin's place on our coach outing on Monday," Helena Winfield confided, and David waited to hear what nasty little surprises Mrs. Franklin (again nobody he knew) had kept in store for her surgeon. (Without a doubt, Mrs. Franklin would be suffering from some rare grave illness and hanging on to life by mere threads.) The best, though, that Mrs. Franklin—who, as it happened, was the woman whom Jocelyn Smith had mentioned to Mrs. Charles during her visit to his office that afternoon—was able to do for her surgeon had been to present him with a positively boring routine broken hip which needed to be set.

"Somebody's always falling over and breaking something or other," Helena Winfield added dismissively. "It's how most of us old ones go in the finish. A sudden fall, pneumonia sets in and that's it . . ."

Sighing inwardly, David glanced in the rearview mirror at

Mrs. Charles, who was now walking back along the road towards her home. Everyone had their cross to bear, he reminded
himself. Even the unflappable Edwina Charles. That brother
of hers would try the patience of a saint!

A car was approaching at speed.

Mrs. Charles stepped quickly from the road on to the verge.
Long green grass brushed wetly against her stockinged legs.
Standing well back against the hedgerow, she waited for the
car to pass.

"Evening, Mrs. Charles," a perky voice said.

She gave a start, looked quickly round.

"Oh, Mr. North," she said, and Stan North popped up on the
other side of the hedgerow. "I didn't see you there," she
added. "You startled me."

"Nice drop of rain we've had today," he remarked. He
stepped through a gap in the hawthorn to stand with her on
the verge. He was not very tall, in his late middle age, and was
wearing a long black mackintosh and muddy wellingtons. His
head was protected by a bright yellow plastic sou'wester. In
his right hand was a bedraggled newspaper.

"Reckon this is yours," he said, handing it to her. "Got your
name on it."

Mrs. Charles took the soggy newspaper between a thumb
and forefinger. "Oh yes, thank you, Mr. North. I wondered
what had become of it. The new delivery boy seems to be having trouble finding out where everyone lives."

"The lazy little perisher probably got tired of looking and
simply chucked it away," he said. "I'd have a word with them
down at the newsagent's about it if I were you."

The road was now clear, and they moved from the verge
and walked on slowly together towards the clairvoyante's bungalow.

"Sad business about Her in post office and Big John, isn't
it?" he went on conversationally. "Who'd have thought it, eh?"
He paused and looked at Mrs. Charles thoughtfully. "You see
a person one day, all happy and smiling, and a few days later,
zzzttl—they're gone."

"Miss Holliday, you mean?" said Mrs. Charles. It was almost impossible to keep anything secret for long in the village, but it wasn't her impression that Stan North had heard that Big John was dead.

He nodded. "She was out with that boy-friend of hers last Sunday afternoon in his car. They were parked on that narrow side-road leading down to the alder marshes. Real girlish she was with him: 'Yes, Mr. Smith . . . no, Mr. Smith . . . you really shouldn't do that, Mr. Smith. . . .' Giggling like a sixteen-year-old, she was. '*Oi, oi!*' I says to myself. 'Best get a move on from here, Stanley my lad, afore things get a bit steamy-like,' if you follow my meaning."

"They didn't know you were there?"

"Did you until I spoke?"

"No," she admitted with a smile.

"Unfortunately, I didn't have much option," he continued. "I suddenly realised they'd see me if I moved. That would've embarrassed all three of us. 'Nothing else for it, Stanley-lad,' I said to myself. 'You'll just have to grit your teeth and think of England.'" He gave the clairvoyante a quick, sidelong look. "Next thing, the car started up and off they went. The boy-friend obviously took the lady at her word when she said he shouldn't oughta. Don't know who was more disappointed," he chuckled. "Him or me! And thereafter, I might say, I looked upon our Miss Holliday in an entirely different light. I mean, who'd have thought she was actually *human* like the rest of us?"

"Who indeed," said Mrs. Charles.

"And now she's dead and gone." He paused, thought for a moment. Then: "There's some as would say the boy-friend's had a lucky escape. But . . . Well—" he shrugged "—who can really say? Happen she was a completely different person from the holy terror we knew."

Arthur Dunphie sat waiting in his car outside the old brewery. Little Gidding's three public houses had been closed for the best part of an hour, and the village had gone to bed for the night. There was no street lighting in the village, and if it hadn't been for a full moon, he would have been sitting in pitch darkness.

While this was not the first time Arthur had seen Little Gidding's most famous landmark late at night, The Brewery still made an eerie sight. It was said to be haunted by the male members of the Fitzsimmons family who had turned a generations-old family recipe for a distinctively flavoured home-brewed ale into a thriving business in the 1850s. The Brewery had closed down some years ago when the last of the male Fitzsimmonses had died out, and the property was now being held in escrow. Nobody seemed to know what was to become of it.

Arthur ducked his head to look at the fragile, lopsided structure and wondered if the Fitzsimmonses' executors and trustees were living in hopes that it would fall down and leave them free to sell off the land to a property developer. That was where the money was, thought Arthur. In the land. Worth a bomb!

He could be saying that about himself tomorrow!

"If you want to hear something to your advantage . . ." That was the message his landlady had given him on his return from Gidding that afternoon. It was strange that the person who had phoned should use that particular expression; and even stranger that only a few hours earlier, the lawyer-friend with whom he had lunched had effectively thrown cold water over those more or less selfsame hopes. Odd, thought Arthur, how one door had closed and another had opened. Though he would rather have heard this something or other to his advantage in broad daylight and elsewhere. But there hadn't been much he could do about that. The caller hadn't left a name or phone number where he could be contacted. And beggars couldn't be choosers. This one certainly couldn't, thought Arthur morosely. Not with the kind of luck he'd been having lately.

He glanced to his right at the public house across the road from The Brewery, the Black Swan. He was to meet his mysterious caller outside The Brewery after closing time at the

Black Swan. An employee, he expected. Somebody who worked there and had overheard something someone had said in the bar. Something to his (Arthur's) advantage; and something about Mae Holliday, of course.

A rather frightening thought suddenly occurred to him. This —the old brewery—wasn't where they met, was it? The local witches' coven?

Arthur ducked his head again and looked at The Brewery. His heart gave a nervous lurch in his breast. Someone was standing in the doorway near the loading bay holding a lighted hurricane-lamp.

This is it! he thought.

CHAPTER 15

Mrs. Charles was thinking about going down to the post-office stores to see Tilly Cockburn when the telephone rang.

She sighed as she went to answer it and hoped it was a client cancelling an appointment with her rather than somebody seeking to make one. The week ahead of her promised to be one of the busiest for some time. Her appointment diary was full, and the mail she had received only a few minutes earlier on behalf of her sick friend, the astrologist, was double the norm for a Monday morning.

The clairvoyante picked up the receiver tentatively. It was Vera Markham, full of apologies for phoning so early in the morning—she hoped she hadn't interrupted anything important—and even more apologetic for having contacted the police following Mrs. Charles's visit to her home on Saturday morning.

"I felt such a fool when the police told me who you were," Mrs. Markham went on without pausing for breath. "I simply didn't connect the name. I'd never have dreamt that *that* Mrs. Charles would visit *me*. I had heard about you, of course." (Not strictly true: it was Mrs. Markham's elderly mother who filled in the blanks left by the police.) "When that poor young girl who worked at those racing stables was murdered a while back and Tarot cards were left lying about everywhere by her killer," she continued. "Anyway, I just rang to say how sorry I am for all the fuss I made and to say I hope it didn't get you into any trouble. I could kick myself for overreacting like that. I've been very much on edge after what happened in the Lady Chapel last week and . . . well, I'm afraid it was that mention of witchcraft in Saturday's papers that did it, put the fear of

God into me. It was stupid, I know, but I really let my imagination run away with me. . . ."

There was a small pause. Then, with a sigh, Mrs. Markham said, "Look . . . I've now drawn my own conclusions as to why you really came to see me. Maybe I'm right and maybe I'm wrong. Ask no questions and you'll be told no lies, as my dear old mother says," she laughed. "And that's really why I've phoned. There's something you might like to know about your client's handkerchief—the one with the forget-me-nots embroidered on it. Call it my peace offering for having been such an idiot on Saturday. I was wrong about them, the forget-me-nots. The handkerchief *was* embroidered with them, and it was one of Mrs. Frearson's. She made it for your client—Mae Holliday—when she (Mae Holliday, that is) was a little girl."

"In Gidding?" asked the clairvoyante with a thoughtful frown.

"Yes. My mother also thought the newspapers were wrong about the forget-me-nots, and so she mentioned it to Mrs. Frearson yesterday afternoon when she went over to visit her at St. Anthony's Village where Mrs. Frearson lives, and Mrs. Frearson told her it was definitely one of hers. She worked the forget-me-nots in the corner specially, because your client was afraid she would forget to send her a handkerchief."

"Mrs. Frearson *sent* it to her?" Mrs. Charles asked slowly. "She didn't actually give or sell it to her in Gidding?"

"Your client visited Gidding on holiday one year with a party of children from a children's home—an orphanage. Mrs. Frearson's memory isn't what it used to be, and she can't remember for sure now where the children came from, but she thinks it was from somewhere in Yorkshire—one of the big industrial towns . . . Bradford or Leeds. She said Mae Holliday was an orphan and that altogether there were three little girls in the group which visited the cathedral one day. Naturally, all three of them wanted to buy a memento of their visit, but apparently there were only two Lady Chapel handkerchiefs to go round. Anyhow, Mrs. Frearson got to hear about the third little girl who'd missed out, and she promised to make one specially for her and post it on to her at the holiday camp where the children were staying before they returned home to Bradford, or wherever."

"Did the police contact Mrs. Frearson about the handkerchief?"

"No, I don't think so. There wouldn't have been any need to, would there? The fleur-de-lis worked into the lace-edging told them it was one of hers; and—" Mrs. Markham hesitated. Then: "Well, it wasn't like it was a clue or something to her murderer, was it? They knew who killed her, didn't they? It was only a matter of catching him."

There was a pause. Then, hesitatingly, Mrs. Markham went on: "You knew your client was an orphan, did you?"

"Something of the kind," replied the clairvoyante.

"Oh," said Mrs. Markham. Then, after another pause: "You know about her name, I suppose . . . that they—the people at the children's home—made it up? She was a foundling, left on the home's doorstep, and they called her Mae Holliday because that was when they found her, on a May Spring Bank Holiday. They never found out what her real name was. At least, that's what Mrs. Frearson told my mother."

"Yes, my client told me about her name and how she came by it," said the clairvoyante quietly.

"One way and another she's turning out to be a real woman of mystery, isn't she?" said Mrs. Markham. She hesitated again. Then, haltingly: "Still, they've caught up with her killer now, haven't they? That's something to be thankful for. Well," she said after a slight, somehow expectant pause, "I won't keep you; I'm sure you're very busy. I just thought that after what you'd said about her being your client, you might like to know the full story behind the handkerchief with the forget-me-nots. I thought it was very interesting. . . ."

The village store was open, but the post office was still closed. An official notice signed by the Head Postmaster at Gidding said, ". . . due to circumstances beyond our control."

"If you ask me," said Tilly as she bustled to and fro filling

Mrs. Charles's order, "they're still trying to make up their minds what they are going to do about it."

"What about the young lass Miss Holliday was training?" inquired the clairvoyante.

"Oh, she hasn't had enough experience yet to run things on her own. She's working temporarily in the Crown Post Office in Gidding until they decide what they want to do with her. I personally don't think we'll ever see our post office open again. I haven't heard anything definite, mind, but my guess would be that Mae—Miss Holliday—didn't leave a will; so don't be surprised if it's bad news all round."

Tilly picked up a short step-ladder and set it down in front of the shelfing behind the counter. Mounting the steps, she reached out for a jar of French mustard at the back of one of the higher shelves and said, "Arthur Dunphie was in here early on Saturday morning nosing around to see what he could find out. . . . You know, about Miss Holliday's will—if she left one. 'You tell me,' I told him."

She climbed back down from the ladder and then dragged it out of the way with her free hand. "You can bet I'll be the last person to be told whether or not I'm out of a job," she said cheerfully. "It won't be so bad now for the village if the store closes down—not like it would've been a few years ago; but if the post office goes, it'll be nothing short of disastrous."

Tilly paused, her eyes widened expressively. "I've always suspected that Agatha Dunphie had good reason for leaving things the way she did, but it looks like she might've made a mistake after all. Though I'm sure Arthur wouldn't have wanted to hang on to it—the store. As Miss Sayer said (she was in here on Saturday morning when he stopped by), running a post office and a grocery store would be too much like hard work for our Arthur. And then when he said he had a lunch appointment in Gidding with his solicitor to discuss the validity of his aunt's will in the light of that black magic movie mentioned in Saturday's paper—I think he was hoping that he could make some sort of claim on Miss Holliday's estate and say she'd used witchcraft on his aunt to make her leave every-

thing to her instead of him—Miss Sayer snapped back at him
that there was no betting shop in the village, so she supposed
that meant he planned on opening one up here in his aunt's—I
mean, Miss Holliday's—store.

"Miss Sayer really is the rudest person," Tilly went on
laughingly. "Not that Arthur minded. That one can give as
good as he gets. He just grinned and said he wouldn't be seen
dead in a betting shop, let alone running one. He always
phoned his bets through to his turf accountant, he said. All the
same though, I think she gave him some food for thought. He
seemed to think about it, as if opening a betting shop in the
village mightn't be a bad idea."

"But first get your shop premises," said Mrs. Charles,
smiling.

"Exactly," said Tilly. "And there's no way Miss Holliday
would've left this little lot to him. Come to think of it, I don't
know who she'd leave it to, unless it was to that Mr. Smith."
She smiled ruefully. "I might've made a mistake there,
mightn't I? Introducing them to one another. In a manner of
speaking, that is. Specially if it ends up costing me my job. I
can't see Mr. Smith suddenly wanting to become a storekeeper.
Not if what people say about him is true. I hear he's utterly
dedicated to his work at St. Anthony's Village, lives and
breathes the place twenty-four hours a day."

"You knew Miss Holliday was keeping steady company with
him, did you?"

"No, not really. But I knew, guessed, there was someone—a
man—in her life. As far as I was concerned, Mr. Smith was just
someone who'd chanced to come into the store one day asking
for directions. He mightn't have even met Mae if it hadn't
been for the fact that I didn't know the people he was trying to
find. They were newcomers—living over in the new housing
development—though I didn't know that then. I had to call
across to Mae—Miss Holliday," Tilly corrected herself, "and
ask her where they lived, and that, apparently, was when
cupid's arrow struck. It'd been going on under my nose ever
since. Miss Holliday never discussed their friendship with me:

we weren't on those terms. She wasn't that type, anyway, was she?"

Mrs. Charles agreed. "When did you first suspect that she had a close man-friend?"

"Thinking back . . . I mean, now that I know about Mr. Smith and her—about three weeks ago. She suddenly seemed . . . well, absent-minded." Tilly grinned. "Moonstruck. And that wasn't a bit like her."

"But they'd been keeping company for much longer than that."

"Yes. For well over a year, by all accounts."

"Maybe there was someone else," the clairvoyante suggested.

"Another man?" Tilly chuckled. "I find it remarkable enough that Mae Holliday had *one* man, let alone two! Unless it was Rafe Curry," she said with a mischievous twinkle in her eye. "She used to blush like mad when he came in. I really think she fancied him. In her own peculiar way."

They turned to the subject of Big John Little's suicide.

Tilly sympathetically shook her head and said, "His poor old dad's simply carrying on as if nothing's happened. Though I guess," she sighed, "after having already buried a wife and three other sons, he probably sees it as just another death in the family, one more funeral to attend."

Mrs. Charles paid for her purchases; then, turning to leave, she said, "Where's Miss Dunphie's clock?"

Tilly looked quickly across at the tiled pillar in the centre of the store.

"Good heavens," she said. "D'you know, I never noticed. It's gone."

Miss Sayer was on her way down to the Day Centre to advise the supervisor that later in the morning she would be going on a coach outing organised by the superintendent of St. Anthony's Village, and that she would not be present for lunch. It was not absolutely essential that she should report in this way, but she usually did so, if for no other reason than to ensure that everyone down there knew that she had something unusual planned for the day which did not include any of them.

She turned down the side of The Brewery, stopped short. The door which gave on to the loading bay was wide open. Again! She tut-tutted under her breath. It was about time the trustees of the Fitzsimmons estate got off their backsides and came down and had a look at what was happening to the place. They were just asking for children to get in and climb all over the machinery, throw bricks through windows, write crude graffiti all over the walls with those wretched cans of spray-paint . . . it was absolutely disgraceful!

She bustled up the stone steps to close the door, which opened out on to a wide platform in the loading bay. Her thoughts rushed on ahead of her: maybe somebody, children, had already broken in and smashed up the place. All the steam-driven machinery was still there. Nothing, to her knowledge, had been sold.

She paused for a moment, then cautiously stepped inside the building.

It was many years since Miss Sayer had been inside The Brewery, and almost as many years since any beer had been brewed in its huge wooden vats, though the smell of yeast and hops was as strong and fresh as if it had been only yesterday that its always immaculately maintained machinery had operated at full steam.

"Disgraceful!" she said out loud as she looked about her at the dust and cobwebs everywhere.

She was in the dispatcher's office off the loading bay.

No sign of any vandalism here.

She saw the hurricane-lamp on the desk, but failed to notice the dust-free ring behind it where it had obviously once stood, and judging by the depth of dust on the perimeter of the ring, for some considerable time.

A wide, latticed window on the far side of the dispatcher's office overlooked some machinery, Miss Sayer thought she could recall from a previous visit. If she remembered correctly, there would be a narrow catwalk beyond the door at the side of the window, and a steep iron staircase with open treads—the sort she didn't like.

The window was too dusty and dirty to see through, so she opened the dispatcher's door and looked out.

The catwalk was still there, and the staircase.

But where was the machinery?

She frowned, looked all round. Even up at the beamed roof. No machinery.

It must have been sold.

Nobody had told her!

She stepped out of the dispatcher's office on to the catwalk, looked down at the great expanse of floor below.

A small cry escaped her lips and she teetered forward, grabbed the iron safety railing. Then, recovering herself, she frowned irritably. Arthur Dunphie was lying on his back in the middle of the floor. And somebody—Arthur himself, she had no doubt—had drawn a wide white chalk circle around him, inside which was a five-pointed star, a pentacle. Miss Sayer recognised the nature of the cabalistic symbols which had been drawn on the points of the pentacle and knew its correct name.

On Arthur's chest was Agatha Dunphie's clock. Arthur's hands were clasping it close to his breast. Something—Miss Sayer had to screw up her eyes to focus them properly on it—was lying on the floor just outside the chalk-drawn circle. A scrap of furry white cloth. No. . . .

She looked harder.

That was . . .

A dead mouse?

A child's pet white mouse!

She looked back at Arthur.

His eyes were wide open and he was looking directly at her. He smiled.

"I know it's you down there, Arthur Dunphie," she called down to him crossly. "I've got eyes in my head!"

Arthur continued to smile at her.

"I'll soon wipe that smile off your face, my boy," she promised him vengefully.

She stormed back through the dispatcher's office, then marched across the platform in the loading bay and stomped down the steps.

She was absolutely fizzing, furious.

Tilly spotted her through the store-window, the expression on Miss Sayer's face leaving her in no doubt that there had been something wrong with the slice of bacon she had sold Miss Sayer on Saturday morning, and that the old lady was on her way back to complain.

"If you're looking for Agatha Dunphie's clock, that fool Arthur's got it down in The Brewery," announced Miss Sayer as she exploded through the door.

Tilly knew that Arthur had taken the clock; that is, he had intimated to her on Saturday morning when he had called in that this was his intention. Miss Holliday had told him that he could take it, and he had given Tilly to understand that he might as well have it. "Who knows," he'd said, "it might be worth a bob or two. American tourists go mad for this kind of thing, don't they?"

Tilly hadn't actually seen him taking the clock down from the pillar, but once Mrs. Charles had drawn her attention to the fact that it was missing, she had assumed that he must have done so while she had slipped out to the stock-room to cut Miss Sayer four ounces of cheddar cheese. Obviously, this was not the case; otherwise Miss Sayer would not have bothered to call in and report its present whereabouts. Tilly did not know for sure, but she imagined that Arthur still had keys to both the store and Rose Cottage, and she guessed that he must have called back there—probably on Sunday when the store was closed—letting himself in with his own key, and taken the clock. Perhaps this was one of the things he had asked his solicitor on Saturday—whether he still had the right. . . .

"What on earth is Arthur doing in The Brewery?" she asked, her eyes widening.

"It's no use asking me," snapped Miss Sayer. "Nobody ever tells me anything. When did they sell the machinery?" she demanded to know.

"Months ago," said Tilly. "Some museum bought it . . . one of those places that specialise in old steam-driven machinery. What about Miss Dunphie's clock? Did Arthur say what he was doing with it in there?"

"He did not! Nor did I ask," said Miss Sayer indignantly. "I had no intention of talking to him while he was in that condition."

"What do you mean?"

"Rolling about drunk on the floor, acting like an overgrown child, drawing childish black magic symbols all over everything . . . I'm not wasting my good time talking to someone in that state."

Tilly gave her a puzzled look.

"Are you quite sure Arthur was drunk, Miss Sayer?"

"What? You think I don't know a drunkard when I see one!"

"Arthur Dunphie doesn't drink," said Tilly. "Tomato juice, or a plain tonic water—that's all he'll ever order when he goes into a public house. He became allergic to alcohol after he had a holiday in Majorca one time and picked up some nasty tummy-bug. Beer and spirits make him seriously ill . . . like penicillin does to some people."

"Rubbish," said the old lady. "He was right as pie—except for the drink, that is—when I saw him a few minutes ago. Laughing all over his face."

"I think you might be mistaken about that, Miss Sayer," said Tilly with a slow shake of her head. "I remember Miss Holliday telling me once how ill alcohol makes Arthur. And you know she wasn't the world's most sympathetic person. If she said something made someone ill, you can be sure of it."

The old lady's eyes steadily widened into a fixed stare.

She could see Arthur Dunphie's round, unblinking gaze, the smile fastened on his lips.

He had been a funny colour too. Sort of waxen.

Miss Sayer opened and shut her mouth.

Arthur Dunphie wasn't drunk.

He wasn't even ill.

He was dead.

Miss Sayer's eyelids fluttered, closed. Tilly could see what was going to happen, but with her great bulk, she was unable to get out from behind the counter in time.

The old lady fell in a limp heap on the floor.

CHAPTER 16

Bright sunshine streamed suddenly through the sitting-room window and into the clairvoyante's eyes, and she rose and adjusted the curtains to cut down on the glare. She turned as David spoke.

"You've heard about Arthur Dunphie, I suppose," he said. "My aunt found him early this morning in The Brewery. He's dead—murdered, the police suspect, though that's not official. Nobody knows for certain yet exactly how he died. I've just left my aunt. Her doctor wanted to put her in hospital. She collapsed in the village store soon after she'd found Dunphie." Wearily, he wiped a hand across an eye and then down the side of his face and around his chin. "God only knows what she was doing in The Brewery. The mind boggles!" he sighed. "Anyhow, she wouldn't hear of it, going into hospital. That friend of hers who came over to tea on Saturday—Helena Winfield—has volunteered to stay with her for a few days. I'm on my way now to fetch her."

Mrs. Charles sat down again and frowned. "I saw the police cars go past shortly before lunch. I naturally thought it was something to do with Big John." She shook her head. "I hadn't heard about Arthur Dunphie." She hesitated. Then, distantly: "I was in the store early this morning. It must've all happened soon after I left."

"I've an idea Dunphie might've been down in the woods on Saturday night, and it doesn't look to me like it was any Teddy bears' picnic he stumbled across," said David wryly. "Tilly Cockburn told the police that he was snooping about in the store on Saturday morning asking questions, and I rather think he might've got his answers, though not from her. Mae Holliday was mixed up with a local witches' coven all right, Madame. Dunphie's murder proves it for me. He was left lying on his back on The Brewery floor inside a chalk-drawn pentacle with the old railway clock from his late aunt's store on his chest—you'll remember that I told you there was a similar clock featured in the black magic movie Mae Holliday was toting about with her when she was murdered—and there was a dead white mouse on the floor just outside the pentacle. The dead mouse is apparently meant to be of some special significance, but it'll be a while before the police can get round to having it checked out."

"I know Agatha Dunphie's clock didn't work—or it wasn't working the last time I looked at it—but what time was it? Where were the hands pointing when the police found Arthur Dunphie?"

"To one o'clock. The hands on the clock in the Mae Holliday movie pointed to a few minutes to midnight, then to midnight itself. Or noon, midday, depending on what period of the day or night the movie was intended to cover. In Dunphie's case, I'd say it was 1 A.M. The police doctor reckons Dunphie'd been dead at least twenty-four hours, probably longer. So it would seem he was definitely killed sometime late on Saturday night or early Sunday morning."

The clairvoyante nodded thoughtfully. "The dead mouse might have been used in a Black Mass. Or I should say, a medieval form of the Black Mass. The mouse is for Lucifer, a gift. It's tossed to him one hour after midnight by the priest conducting the Black Mass. . . ." She hesitated, frowned. "Though with this older form of the Black Mass, it was an ordained priest of the Church of Rome who would officiate, one who secretly worshipped Satan." Her eyes narrowed. "I can't quote you chapter and verse. It's quite some while ago now that I read about it—in a book on witchcraft I came across in some dark forgotten corner of my brother's study (and I seem to remember that he said it wasn't his, it had been left behind by the previous occupiers of his house). However, I think it would be reasonably safe to assume that Arthur Dunphie's dead mouse was a ritual sacrificial offering to Satan."

"And a damn sight cheaper than a goat. Even a chicken these days," said David wryly. "Dunphie's neck was broken. How, the police don't yet know. But it's possible he fell—or was pushed—from a catwalk beyond the old dispatcher's office in The Brewery and broke his neck when he landed on the floor below. It's also possible that he was struck on the back of the head . . ." David's voice tailed off into a long drawn-out sigh, implicit in which was the suggestion that Big John Little was somehow involved in this latest killing.

The clairvoyante looked at him steadily. "The police surely don't think Big John Little killed him?" Her eyes widened. "But how? Arthur Dunphie was alive around noon on Saturday—I spoke to him personally in Gidding: he was on his way to keep a luncheon appointment with his solicitor."

"I know, I know," he said with another sigh. He made a small dismissive gesture with his hand. "Big John was already dead. He'd been dead for hours. He couldn't possibly have killed him. But maybe his old man could've. . . ."

He shook his head at the look of incredulity on the clairvoyante's face. "One doesn't need to be possessed of the physical strength and vigour of Hercules to kill somebody with a blow to the back of the head, Madame," he pointed out soberly. "Not if you know what you're doing. And even I've got to admit that Big John was taught everything he knew about killing—animals, that is—by his old man. The old boy was just as deadly in his day. And what's more, he enjoyed it and had a reputation for enjoying it. There was a time—many years ago now, of course—when Little John's kills would be the main topic of conversation down at the Black Swan of a night. Merton's not taken me into his confidence, Madame, but he's having Little John brought in for questioning, and my impression is that the interrogation won't be confined solely to Dunphie's murder. Merton's been puzzled all along by Little John's reaction to Big John's suicide. He was a little too complacent about it all for Merton's liking."

"And you, Superintendent? What do you feel about it?"

He frowned. "I'm not sure. I confess that at the time it seemed that he was rather more stoic than one would perhaps have expected in the circumstances. But then he's of that tough old breed who don't show their emotions. His generation was brought up in hard times: they had nothing and expected nothing, accepted life as it was dished out to them and made the most of it without whining about their lot. But now, as I've said, I'm not so sure. Merton might be on to something. I doubt that Big John was a witch, a member of some local coven. His fondness for the hard stuff would've made him too great a risk. A few drinks and he couldn't keep anything a secret—and he would've relished bragging about something like that. But I can see his father belonging to a witches' coven —and killing Mae Holliday. Not because of the trouble over the Littles' pensions, but because of some transgression she'd committed against the coven. And I can also see him acting on orders from the coven and killing Dunphie because he got too nosy and perhaps came perilously close to discovering the truth about what's been going on in the village. I know he's a very old man, Madame, but he's both mentally and physically tough, the wiry kind that seems to go on forever. He'll still be piling withies into that old boiler of his as the hearse draws up to cart him off to his own funeral. . . ."

"I should've thought all writing materials—paper, pen and ink, or a piece of chalk—would be anathema to an illiterate," observed the clairvoyante quietly.

"I take your point, Madame," said David. "However, I very much doubt that Little John drew the pentacle and the cabalistic signs on The Brewery floor—not unless he's been pretending all these years about not being able to read and write, which isn't very likely. They were extremely well drawn—I would've said by the hand of a highly educated person. And this can only mean that Little John wasn't alone when he murdered Dunphie. The other members of the coven were in on the kill, and one of them drew the pentacle and the rest of it."

"And The Brewery was their meeting place?"

"It looks that way. Heaven only knows how long it would've been before Dunphie's body was discovered if it hadn't been for my aunt." David's eyebrows rose. "It's certainly taken the wind out of her sails, I can tell you. I've never known her to have so little to say." He looked quickly at the time. "Which reminds me . . . I must be going. My aunt's friend will be wondering what's become of me."

He hesitated and the clairvoyante smiled.

"No, Superintendent," she said, anticipating the question he was about to ask. "No news yet. I still haven't got any answers."

She didn't say so, but with her present work-load, she doubted that she would be able to do much more about the matter before the weekend. And she was still trying to pin Cyril down for that talk about the Lady Chapel. That in itself was going to be no mean feat; it could take weeks!

CHAPTER 17

The clairvoyante crossed the sweeping, shrub-filled lawn at the front of the Linthorpes' sprawling Cotswold stone and red-brick bungalow, one of the larger bungalows in a curving cul-de-sac of fifteen in what was still referred to as "the new housing development" even though it had been part of the village now for over ten years. This was where most of "the newcomers"—wealthy retired city folk like Professor Linthorpe and his wife Rosemary—preferred to live. The Linthorpes came to Little Gidding in March after losing another property—the one they had really wanted to buy—in a tiny hamlet only a few miles outside the town of Gidding.

All week it had been chilly, for the most part with steady grey skies, but it was slowly warming up again, and the sky at the moment was a pale hazy blue.

Nothing stirred, neither within the bungalow after Mrs. Charles had knocked on the door, nor in any of its surrounding garden. There was nobody else about, but from further up the road came the sound of a motor mower which died away as the clairvoyante knocked once more on the door.

She waited a few minutes longer, then turned away and started back across the lawn. The Linthorpes could have gone into Gidding on a shopping expedition—a popular Saturday afternoon activity with many of the villagers. They might even have been amongst the handful of spectators sitting in distant deck-chairs watching the cricket match which had been in progress on the village green as the clairvoyante had walked past, though she remembered Mrs. Linthorpe telling her once that the professor preferred playing bowls with some chums of his in Gidding to watching local village cricket teams playing

their "dreary Saturday and Sunday afternoon matches," as
Mrs. Linthorpe had called them.

Mrs. Charles decided to try the library instead. The professor was the author of at least one book that she knew of on
British folk customs, possibly more, and the library was almost
certain to have copies of anything he had written, especially as
he was a local resident.

The clairvoyante heard her brother coming long before she
could actually see him. She was halfway across the Linthorpes'
neatly shaved lawn when the leather-jacketed motor-cyclist—
her brother, Cyril—finally zoomed past her, braked, circled
once in the middle of the road, and then rode slowly back to
where she was standing at the roadside watching him.

Cyril pulled up, removed his red crash-helmet, and tucked it
under his arm.

"I thought it was you," he said. "What are you doing over
here?"

"I was hoping to have a word with Professor Linthorpe, but
no one appears to be at home."

"I saw him loading up that caravan of his earlier on," said
Cyril. "It looked to me as if he and his wife were going away
for some while. He probably wants to get away from it all. I
overheard him saying in the Black Swan last night that he'd
never have come here to live if he'd known it was going to be
like this, and that he and his wife would sell up and move back
to the city and get a bit of peace and quiet if it weren't for all
the expense of uprooting themselves again so soon after their
last move."

"I didn't think Professor Linthorpe got all that involved
with what goes on in the village."

"It's pretty hard not to, isn't it? What with people getting
themselves murdered and what have you. He seemed thor-
oughly fed up with the lot of it last night . . . only stayed for
one drink."

"How very inconvenient for him," said Mrs. Charles dryly.
"What did you want to see him about?"

"I wondered if his knowledge of British folk customs included witchcraft."

"Somebody buttonholed him about that last night in the pub. There's a book of Linthorpe's in the library on witchcraft, and this bloke was quizzing him about it, really bending his ear. That was when Linthorpe jacked it in and cleared off. Couldn't say I blamed him. This other chap wasn't terribly bright, asked some really stupid questions."

Cyril put on his crash-helmet, revved up his bike.

"Since when have you been interested in witchcraft?" he shouted at his sister over the din of his machine.

"Since Mae Holliday was murdered."

He adjusted the visor on his helmet, used the throttle. The engine roared, then faded.

"You're off to the library, then," he guessed. "You could be wasting your time. There'll be a mile-long waiting list to borrow Linthorpe's witchcraft book now."

"What for?" asked Mrs. Charles.

"Same reason you want to look at it, I expect. Everyone now wants to know what it's all about, don't they? The pentacle drawn round Dunphie—that's what the bloke in the Black Swan last night was curious about. And that home-made movie of Mae Holliday's."

"Professor Linthorpe's book won't tell them anything about that, not unless they've seen the film."

He thought about it, shrugged. "Then why are you wasting your time with him?"

"Because I know what's in it."

"Oh," he said. He nodded, the bike rolled forward. It covered about ten yards, then Cyril circled slowly while he waited for his sister to catch up to him.

"What's it all about?"

"I don't know, Cyril," she said patiently. "That's why I'm here, isn't it? I'm hoping to see Professor Linthorpe and ask him if he can tell me what it all means."

He looked at her. "You've seen the film?"

"No, but David Sayer has."

Cyril narrowed his eyes. "Does that mean it's one of your little secrets and you're not to tell me?"

It had been many years since David Sayer, as Detective Chief Superintendent Sayer, had taken an active interest in some of Cyril's more bizarre UFO exploits, but Cyril still liked to feel aggrieved about it, and particularly about the night he had spent in the cells at the Chief Superintendent's exasperated behest.

Mrs. Charles described the content of the home-made movie to her brother.

He listened, nodded again, then rolled his bike forward for several yards, revved up the engine, and rode off.

His sister caught up with him again outside her bungalow, where he was riding round and round in circles in the middle of the road waiting for her. She had abandoned her plan to visit the library. Cyril was sure to be right about a waiting list for the professor's book on witchcraft. She could probably research and write one of her own on the subject in the time it would take for her turn to come round to borrow his.

"What makes you think that's black magic, witchcraft?" Cyril asked her curiously, picking up their conversation from where it had been left off some fifteen minutes earlier.

She looked at him thoughtfully. "Isn't it?"

He shrugged, toyed for a moment or two with the throttle on his machine. "Can't think where you got that idea. Sounds more to me like the ringing of the Devil's Knell."

"So?" she said.

"The Devil's Knell hasn't got anything to do with witchcraft, devil worship," said Cyril. "It's the exact opposite, the complete reverse."

The clairvoyante walked slowly up the path and let herself in. Arthur Dunphie had been right, of course. Being a witch, a member of a coven—a member of anything—would've taken a far greater personal commitment than Mae Holliday would ever have been capable of giving. She was a confirmed loner.

There had been no desecration of the Lady Chapel. There

was no witches' coven, certainly not in the village. There never had been—not in recent times, anyway. It was all an extension of the one big original lie, a spin-off from the lie Mae Holliday had been living these past sixteen years. A lie compounded by more lies.

As Mrs. Charles started to make herself a cup of tea, she pondered on the comment Jocelyn Smith had made to her shortly before she had left his office the previous Saturday afternoon, that every misfortune which befell one had its purpose, there were no errors. . . .

She had understood, could even sympathise with these sentiments, which were something of her own philosophy of life; however, she was no longer able to agree with him that a time would come when he could look back on this tragic episode in his life and say, in all truthfulness, that there were no errors, that all things had worked for the final good of those concerned. In this instance, there *were* errors, mistakes which, like the lie Mae Holliday had told herself, had been compounded time and again by more mistakes. Those Mae Holliday had made. Those the police had made. Those Arthur Dunphie had made. Her own. Someone had certainly led them one and all the Devil's own dance.

The clairvoyante abruptly stopped what she was doing and gazed the length of her long garden to the wood running along the bottom of it. Her blue eyes darkened. She heard Mae Holliday's voice . . . "Needs must when the Devil drives."

Mae Holliday had tried to remember who had spoken those words to her. Someone from the past. . . .

The clairvoyante's gaze intensified. Yes, there were mistakes. And someone had made a really big one this time which she had once again very nearly compounded by what would have been the biggest mistake of all.

She cast her mind back. . . .

Everything Mae Holliday had said to her that Wednesday afternoon concerning her predicament—whether true or false—had been of some relevance and had been treated by her as such. Except for that one remark. It hadn't even struck her as

being odd—as it did now—that Mae Holliday had not simply
said "Needs must" (which was all most people said) and left it
at that.

Mrs. Charles frowned reflectively. "Needs must when the
Devil drives" was the modern phraseology of the aphorism.
This was not its original form. Not if she remembered correctly
from her school-days.

She switched off the kettle and went into her small consult-
ing-room, removed a book from one of the shelves lining the
walls, then carried it to her desk, shifted some papers aside,
and sat down. She opened the book, found what she was looking for, read for a moment, then got up and took down another
book, looked at the contents, then returned with it to her desk.

Turning to the page she wanted, she glanced over it and
then, skipping two more pages, she began to read.

A heaviness settled on her. She finished reading, closed the
book, and leaned back in her chair. It was some minutes before
she stirred; then she reached for the telephone, hesitated momentarily, frowned, and finally picked up the receiver and
dialled David Sayer's number.

He answered the phone on the third ring, responded (some-
what pawkily) to the clairvoyante's preliminary inquiries concerning his aunt's present state of health—"She's found her
voice again," he said; a sure sign that she was well on the road
to recovery—and then Mrs. Charles said:

"When you called on me last Monday afternoon and told me
about Arthur Dunphie and your aunt, you intimated that she'd
had very little to say about what had happened to him, and yet
presumably she saw him exactly as he was later found by the
police. Had she nothing at all to say about the pentacle, or the
clock and the dead mouse?"

Puzzled, David replied, "The only comment she made—to
me, that is—was that she thought Dunphie was drunk and
playing silly beggars. I don't know what she said to the police.
Very little, I would suspect, that was coherent."

"Did you see him before he was moved?"

"Yes."

"What was your reaction?"

He hesitated. "To what I saw?" He thought about it. "Well, strange as it may seem, much the same as my aunt's. When one looked down on Dunphie from the catwalk, which must be all of twenty feet above the floor he was lying sprawled out on, that was exactly how it looked, as if the silly devil was acting the goat. Deliberately trying to scare someone. It was somehow unreal. You felt as if you wanted to call down to him to cut it out and stop behaving like an overgrown kid."

"Is that how you felt when you watched the Mae Holliday movie?"

David hesitated again, even more puzzled now. "No," he said slowly. "Now, that's odd, isn't it? The movie was definitely faked, make-believe—the mock-up of the church and the coffin —and yet it was . . . well, something about the way the whole thing was done made it so disturbing that one forgot it wasn't real. Perhaps, simply, because a small child was involved, or maybe because one instinctively realised that the mind of the person behind the camera was sick, twisted."

There followed such a long silence that David had to ask if the clairvoyante were still there on the line.

Then she said: "Those answers you wanted, Superintendent. I think the time has come for us to have a long talk. . . ."

CHAPTER 18

David apologised for his lateness. It was over three hours since the clairvoyante had telephoned him, and it was now well after nine o'clock and growing dark.

"I came as soon as I could," he went on. "Aunt Margaret took a sudden turn for the worse not two minutes after you'd rung off. I don't think that Helena Winfield was such a good idea after all. She's not been anywhere near firm enough with the old lady. She let her have far too many visitors today, and it's all been a bit too much for her. We're keeping our fingers crossed and hoping it's just another attack of the vapours. Aunt Margaret's prone to them, particularly when she's been wrong about something and people keep calling round and reminding her of it. Some of these old dears use their tongues like lethal rapiers and give no quarter to anyone. Which is all very well, but the old lady's got a dicky ticker now—she can't take it like she used to—and if she hasn't calmed down by the time I leave here, Jean thinks it's best to be on the safe side; Aunt Margaret should go into hospital and no ifs and buts about it!"

"I'm sorry," said Mrs. Charles. "I'm being very selfish." She stirred from the sofa where she had been sitting, for the most part in semi-darkness, waiting for him, and switched on a table-lamp. "I'm sure Jean would need you to be with her. This can wait."

"Maybe so. But I can't," he said with a smile. "I'm dying of curiosity. Jean can handle my aunt much better when I'm not there. I only antagonise the old lady. Not to mention getting under everyone's feet!"

He had already observed the wine-table and the five Tarot

cards which were laid out on it, three face down. Inclining his head at the cards, he asked, "What's all this?"

"The reading I did for Mae Holliday," the clairvoyante replied. "We will go into that later. First, there's something else I would like to discuss with you."

He nodded and sat down in the leather armchair near the open fireplace. Mrs. Charles studied him for a moment, then she turned aside and poured two whiskies from a crystal decanter on the sideboard. She handed one to him and then returned with her drink to the sofa and sat down again.

She spoke seriously. "Names will not have been changed to protect the innocent. Any question mark there may be relates solely to events—those subsequent to Mae Holliday's visit here last Wednesday week—mainly because much of what I have to tell you regarding those events has yet to be proved."

She paused and gazed into her glass. "I knew Mae Holliday would come to me for help; in fact, I cancelled all my appointments for the remainder of that particular day in anticipation of her visit."

"Why?" David's eyebrows rose. "Mae Holliday never did anybody any favours."

"All the more reason why I should do her one," the clairvoyante responded quietly.

"You're sure you weren't simply curious?" he asked with a faint smile.

"Even if I didn't have a natural instinct for these things, Mae Holliday's uncharacteristic behaviour while I was in the post office that Wednesday morning would've made it plain to the most insensitive and unobservant of people that she had something on her mind. And by the time I had concluded my business, I knew—as I have already told you—that she would come to see me about it, whatever it was that troubled her. I also knew that she was standing in the shadow of death."

Mrs. Charles levelled a steady gaze at David. Her voice softened, became distant. "Some clairvoyants speak of an aura surrounding someone who is about to die, but it has never been that way for me. The Bible speaks of the valley of the

shadow of death, and this was where Mae Holliday was standing, in the valley of the shadow of death. As I left the post
office that morning, I looked back at her, and I could see its
heavy overhanging shadow. There was nothing anyone could
do about it," she said simply. Then, shaking her head slowly:
"No, Superintendent. I wasn't curious. Anything but. I could
do only one thing for Mae Holliday, one small kindness before
she died, and that was to listen to her when she came to me for
help."

She paused and sighed. "It sounds so simple, doesn't it? You
may even be asking yourself why, when I knew what lay in
store for this poor, wretched woman, was I unable to do anything for her. The answer, quite simply, is as it was then. Mae
Holliday herself. She made it impossible for anybody to help
her. Mae Holliday was a liar, Superintendent. But not your
common everyday liar. She was sick, confused, genuinely unable to sort fact from fiction. She was acting out a fantasy—living a lie and living with a lie. One she had told herself approximately sixteen years ago; and in making herself believe it, she
had created a mental block, a kind of amnesia. As a direct result of this lie, the one she had made herself believe, Mae
Holliday—or rather the woman who *called* herself Mae Holliday . . . the woman we in the village knew as Mae Holliday—
didn't know who she really was. By that I mean who she was
before she came here to work for Agatha Dunphie in the post
office."

"Sounds to me like she needed a psychiatrist, not a clairvoyante," David remarked.

Mrs. Charles nodded. "I would think she'd suffered from
some form of serious mental disturbance since early childhood.
Maybe she was even treated as a child for this psychological
disorder. It isn't impossible. However, to get back to the
present. . . .

"Mae Holliday didn't tell me what was really troubling her.
All she asked of me was that I should read her past for her. She
didn't wish to know what the future held for her. Whereas the
average person's interest lies solely in the present and the fu-

ture, Mae Holliday, as an amnesiac, was understandably completely obsessed with the past. She knew she was suffering
from loss of memory—she'd known it for sixteen years, ever
since she'd made herself believe the big original lie and moved
to the village to live. It was no sudden realisation. It was her
obsession with discovering the truth about her past that was
recent and, I felt, indicated that she was coming out of it, her
amnesia . . . this state of suspended animation, the twilight
life she'd been living—and, I stress, been fully aware of—for
the past sixteen years. She was slowly remembering what it
was that she had made herself forget, who she really was.
Something had happened which had made her turn back and
face the big original lie."

"She'd suffered some kind of shock?"

"Not quite in the way I think you might mean, an abrupt
one. This was something that had crept stealthily up on her
over a certain period of time. She wouldn't tell me why she
needed to know who she really was, just that she believed she
might soon have reason to need this information. Having since
learnt, through you, of her romantic attachment to Jocelyn
Smith, I would think it was this, the proposal of marriage I suspect she might've anticipated from him, which brought about
her urgent desire to know the truth about herself."

David nodded his head. "She thought she might be illegitimate, and she didn't want any nasty surprises at some inconvenient moment . . . when, say, the boy-friend might learn of
it?"

"She said it didn't concern her. Her illegitimacy, that is. If
indeed it proved to be that she was illegitimate. And I don't
believe it did concern her. Not unduly. Subconsciously, she
knew there were much bigger issues in her past for her to con-
tend with than this."

"Like her participation in certain black magic rituals as a
child?"

The clairvoyante looked at him steadily.

"Well?" he asked. "Was she or wasn't she a witch?"

"You're getting way ahead of me, Superintendent." She

paused, smiled fleetingly. "On more than one occasion you have called me devious, and this, I think you'll have to agree, is what I was with Mae Holliday. Principally, I might add in my own defence," she interjected, "because I was so sure in my own mind that she was lying to me. So when she made me promise not to tell her fortune, what lay in the future, I readily agreed. However, I gave no assurances about the card-spread I would use; and knowing nothing of the Tarot, it didn't occur to her that my promise not to tell her anything about the present and the future should also include a guarantee that I wouldn't take a look at both if, at some later date, I felt I should."

Mrs. Charles waved a hand at the cards spread out on the table. "That is why three of those cards are lying face down. The other two—*The Moon* and *Judgment*—represented Mae Holliday's past, and those were the only cards I looked at while she was here."

"Not much for you to go on," he said.

"No. This again representative, I felt, of the lie Mae Holliday was living and had made herself believe. She was still clinging to it, still reluctant to part with it, even though she knew she must. Those two cards, however, told me enough about her past for me to be able to give her quite considerable pause for thought. That, incidentally, was how the matter was left between us. I told her all that I could of her past, then suggested that she should go away and think about what she had learnt and then come back to me again the following day and permit me to look at the present and the future for her, but only in relation to the two cards covering her past. I knew she wouldn't come back, that I would probably never see her again, but she promised that she would think about it."

"What did the two cards tell you?"

"More or less what I've already told you. *The Moon* confirmed that she was a liar—something I already knew, sensed, simply by talking to her—and it also told me that she was deluding herself about something. That something unforeseen, like the crab, or crayfish, you can see hiding in a pool of water in the picture on that card, was lying in wait for her, deceptively hidden from view by the rays of moonlight which lie across the dark water. The howling dogs of that card are a warning of the presence of the crayfish, the big deceiver, which generally—as in Mae Holliday's case—is ignored. The other card, *Judgment*, condemned her for, shall we say, her sins, and promised atonement for them."

"Did you tell her she was a liar?"

"As kindly and gently as I could, yes." The clairvoyante looked at David intently. "I say 'gently' because I was convinced—and *The Moon* confirms it—that she was only partly aware of her self-deception. For the moment, it was only a terribly frightening suspicion that was just beginning to dawn on her. She knew she lied to other people: she'd known that for sixteen years. What she hadn't realised—until then, that is—was that she'd also been lying to herself. Or rather, she *suspected* that she might've been lying to herself, but she had no idea in what way. Her mind was so horribly confused, she couldn't trust it. She needed someone to guide her through the maze in her head and show her where and when her thinking was wrong and how this wrong thinking was deliberately deceiving and confusing her."

Mrs. Charles paused reflectively. Then, absently: "I wonder now what I would've told her—or perhaps I should say, *how much* I'd have told her—had she not tied my hands by insisting that my reading should be confined strictly to the past. Had she permitted me then to look at the whole picture, I could've told her considerably more, enough possibly—that is, if she were fully ready to face up to the lie—to enable her to recall what it was that her brain had refused to allow her to remember."

The clairvoyante sighed a little, then leaning forward, she picked up a card, one of those facing downwards, and turned it over.

"When I look at this card, *The Emperor*, and this card, *The Devil*—" she turned up another card "—which come from the forbidden part of Mae Holliday's reading, the future, and read them in conjunction with *The Moon* and *Judgment*, I can see very clearly that in her distant past, during her childhood, a man—someone she looked up to and respected—took advantage of her."

David frowned. "Sexually?"

"Probably. I would imagine that she was frigid, and this, I think you'll find the sex therapists will agree, could be the reason why, because she was interfered with sexually when she was a child."

David nodded slowly. "Who was it in her case? A close friend of the family? An uncle?"

"*The Emperor* tells me that it could've been her father, but in the light of what little she was able to tell me about herself, I would be more inclined to think that it was someone she saw as a father-figure."

"But I understood you to say that everything she told you was a lie."

"And in every lie she told me, Superintendent, was an element of truth. The difficulty lay in separating the few minute grains of truth from the large dollops of fiction. For example, she told me that Mae Holliday wasn't her real name, that she had made it up. True or false? And the answer? Both true and false. It wasn't her real name, but she didn't make it up. She borrowed it, stole it—whatever you care to call it—on a May Spring Bank Holiday sixteen years ago during which, she said, she went to the housing department of Gidding Town Hall looking for accommodation and was required to give a desk clerk a name. That May holiday was allegedly the inspiration for her name."

"The Town Hall is closed on Bank Holidays."

"Exactly. The first lie. But by the same token, I have no doubt that at some time she did pay a visit to the Town Hall seeking accommodation. She took with her a shoulder-bag (she called it) shaped like a dog. One with spots on it. She said there was some money in it (true), which I would think she had stolen. The shoulder-bag and the money were her sole possessions, she told me. False. According to what you've told me, and what the newspapers say, in addition to the spotted-dog purse, there was the torn cover of an old movie-star magazine with the name "Mae Holliday" written on it, a lace-edged handkerchief with blue forget-me-nots worked in a corner of it, and a home-made movie of a rather dubious nature. The first two items, like the money, were stolen. The magazine cover and the handkerchief were the property of someone else. They belonged to the real Mae Holliday, the person whose name Little Gidding's postmistress had also stolen. And the third item, the reel of movie-film, related to her. That is, to the real Mae Holliday whom I now believe our Miss Holliday impersonated both on film and ultimately in real life."

Mrs. Charles paused. Then, with a slow shake of her head: "Big John Little didn't kill Mae Holliday, Superintendent. I'm sure of it—the cards are sure of it. The man—the father-figure from Mae Holliday's past, the man she had looked up to who'd first taken advantage of her sexually, then later held her in such savage bondage that she eventually suffered a serious mental breakdown . . . a black-out, amnesia—killed her. And the reason he killed her was because of that reel of movie-film. When, finally, the young girl we here in the village knew as Mae Holliday—who would've then, I believe, been about fifteen or sixteen—ran away from home, so to speak—broke free of this evil man's clutches—she took the film, the symbol of her bondage, with her."

"So it does have something to do with witchcraft?"

"No, Superintendent. The police got that wrong too. Though I am in no way criticising them for it. I made the same error. I too thought it was more than likely that Mae Holliday and the man who'd figured so dominantly in her past were, or had been, Satanists, witches. In Mae Holliday's case—as she was only a child at the time—unwillingly. Unfortunately—and particularly for Arthur Dunphie—her killer capitalised on everyone's misconception about the content of the film. Her real killer was delighted with everybody's mistake—probably couldn't believe his good fortune. He wanted everyone to go on believing that there really was a witches' coven meeting secretly somewhere here in the village. You see, Superintendent, he knew that if anyone discovered what that film was really all about, the truth about him and his ugly past would in all probability come out into the open and ruin him."

The clairvoyante paused and looked at David thoughtfully. "Have you ever heard of the ringing of the Devil's Knell?"

He shook his head.

"There is a parish church in West Yorkshire where every year they ring what Cyril, my brother, tells me is known as the Devil's Knell. The tenor bell of this particular church is tolled on Christmas Eve once for every year that has passed since the birth of Christ. And the timing of the ringing of the bell is precise. According to Cyril, it finishes exactly at the stroke of midnight on Christmas Eve. As I understand it, the Devil's Knell is rung to celebrate the birth of Christ and his triumph over sin and the Devil, whose death it also proclaims. The bell used for the ringing of the Devil's Knell is said to have been donated by a medieval sinner—" She smiled. "A man who it's alleged had committed a murder for which he was never tried, and he himself rang the Devil's Knell each Christmas for the remainder of his life in expiation of his sin."

David frowned at her. "And this is what you think the little girl in the movie was doing?"

"To be more precise, what she was being forced *to watch*, Superintendent. As an act of atonement. The man who dominated her life made a mock-up, you said, of a church interior which featured a cheap home-made coffin, some candles for dramatic effect, a big clock, and a circlet of mistletoe because it was Christmas-time—in this instance, the mistletoe wasn't a pagan symbol in the truest sense, part of a witchcraft rite, as most people would've not unnaturally supposed. He then filmed the coffin, which apparently contained the body of a child (and probably, as you've said, the same little girl played both roles). . . ."

Nodding, David said slowly, "And then after the coffin-lid was nailed down, there was a final shot of the clock at midnight, followed by one of a big bell being tolled by the little girl."

"Which, of course, if it were a real bell, as you've suggested," said the clairvoyante, "a child couldn't do. I doubt that she would've had sufficient strength. But she could sit and watch the movie that had been made of her symbolically ringing the Devil's Knell on Christmas Eve for her sins. And I believe she was forced to watch it, over and over again, until finally she could take no more. She broke loose, ran away."

"Whatever could she have done to warrant that kind of treatment?"

"I think you'll find the answer to that lies with the dead child she was forced to impersonate . . . a foundling who was given the name of *Mae Holliday* because she was left on the doorstep of a children's home on a May Spring Bank Holiday."

"How on earth do you know all this?" David asked, stunned.

"The handkerchief, Superintendent—the one with the forget-me-nots. The old lady who made it specially for the real Mae Holliday told me—indirectly, that is, through Vera Markham."

The clairvoyante smiled solemnly. "Yes, Superintendent. Another mistake. The handkerchief was a further clue as to the true identity of the killer of Little Gidding's postmistress."

She paused, narrowed her eyes musingly. "The home-made movie tells us that we can safely assume that our Miss Holliday was in some way responsible for the real Mae's death. And I would think that the real Mae died probably as a result of some injury to the back of her head . . . roughly where our Miss Holliday told me she'd suffered a head injury (which she hadn't, of course—this was just one of the many lies she'd made herself believe), and where, the next day in the Lady Chapel of Gidding Cathedral, her killer deliberately struck her. Atonement, Superintendent, as the Tarot card *Judgment* suggests. An eye for an eye. And a bad mistake on her killer's part. Yes—" she nodded "—he's made them too. Though this was by no means his biggest. His worst mistake was yet to come . . . when he told me he was the dominant father-figure in the fraudulent Mae Holliday's life, who came out of her twilight past like the deceptive crayfish in the picture on the Tarot card in her reading, and killed her."

David stared at her. Then, shaking his head: "We're never going to prove all this, Madame."

She looked at him. "You don't think so?"

CHAPTER 19

Detective Chief Superintendent Clive Merton looked across his desk at David Sayer, his heavy eyebrows meeting over a purposely bored, unblinking gaze. "And what," he asked, "about the witnesses who saw Big John Little in St. Anthony's Square?"

"Big John went back and forth across the cathedral square to the Bishop's Mitre every market-day around that time, between twelve noon and one o'clock."

"And last Thursday week," the Chief Superintendent shot back at him irritably, "he made a slight detour through the Lady Chapel. But," he sighed, "I know I won't get any peace until you've had your full say." He swept a hand back over his balding scalp in an exasperated gesture, then leaned back resignedly in his chair and said, "Very well, then. Why hang himself if he was innocent?"

"Because he'd had enough, wanted out," replied David simply. "For years he'd been the butt of village jokes, and he was fed up with it, sick of being the village buffoon, the lazy layabout who was always good for a laugh after you'd got a few bevvies into him and he started swaggering about and bragging. Only he wasn't funny, not really. He was pathetic. And he knew it. The village idiot who couldn't even write his name. How was someone like that, someone who could only barely communicate with his fellow man, other than when he was blind drunk, convince anyone—particularly the police—that he hadn't killed the woman whom everyone knew had publicly humiliated him? He'd already been the victim of some pretty rough police justice, been set upon by men and dogs for something he hadn't done—and that was for only a minor offence, a bit of petty thieving. This was murder."

David slowly shook his head. "Big John was the great red stag which chooses to kill itself rather than be run to ground by the huntsman and his dogs. When the river began to rise and the marshes flooded, he headed for home, talked things over with his old dad, then went down the back to the withy shed to get drunk and brood. For him this was the final round in the never ending battle he'd always had to fight in order to survive. He couldn't win, but at least he could lose on his own terms."

"You won't believe this, Clive," David went on, "I could scarcely believe it myself—" he frowned "—but it was there in the cards—the Tarot reading Edwina Charles did for Mae Holliday. Mrs. Charles knew that Big John was going to hang himself; she knew you'd never take him alive. She showed me the very card that represented him and his involvement in Mae Holliday's murder, explained how it all tied in with the things she could see in the cards for Mae Holliday, and even I could see that he was going to hang himself."

"Where's all this leading us, Dave—?" Merton breathed wearily. "You want us to go back to the witnesses and start all over again, is that it?"

"Not those witnesses," said David. "You were looking in the wrong place. Mae Holliday's killer didn't use the square. He picked his way unnoticed through the piles of rubbish in the alley-way linking Monks Lane with the cloisters. That's how he gained access to the cathedral—through the cloisters, not the square."

"Like some sort of spider-man who can scale walls. Or maybe he's Father Christmas and he came down the chimney," Merton suggested bitingly.

"Neither. He did the sensible thing and used a door. Just like anybody else. The one to the Lady Chapel."

"Which is kept locked from the inside," Merton reminded him.

"Maybe he slipped into the cathedral earlier in the day and

unlocked it. Or maybe," said David after a slight pause, "he simply knocked on the door and Mae Holliday, who was expecting him, unlocked it and let him in."

"Just like that," said Merton laconically.

"Ask Vera Markham what she was dreaming about shortly before she woke up and went and took a look in the Lady Chapel."

Merton stared at him. "You're not serious, I hope?"

"Edwina Charles is. Dead serious."

"She would be," said Merton bleakly. "So what was Vera Markham dreaming about?"

"She told Mrs. Charles she heard someone knocking . . . words to that effect."

Merton looked unimpressed. "Go on."

"Vera Markham said it was St. Anthony—in her dream, of course," said David quickly when the Chief Superintendent gave him a hard look. "But Mrs. Charles thinks it could've been Mae Holliday's killer—and I'm not talking about Big John Little—either knocking on the Lady Chapel door for Mae Holliday to let him in, or making a bit of a racket when he killed her, and that Vera Markham wove what she'd subconsciously heard into her dream and got everything jumbled up, the way we do when we're only dozing and not fast asleep."

The Chief Superintendent looked pointedly at his watch. "I don't like to hurry you, Dave, but I'm a bit pushed for time this morning. D'you think you could get to the point? What are you—or should I say, Edwina Charles—really after? You both know I'm going to need a whole lot more than something someone might or might not have heard while they were dreaming to make me change my mind about Big John Little."

"Who shot the film you found on Mae Holliday?" David asked abruptly.

Merton scowled at him. "And just what exactly d'you think I've been doing these past ten days?"

David raised his eyebrows. "You know who made it?"

"No, of course I damn well don't," growled Merton. "Ask me again after I've found Arthur Dunphie's killer."

"You've let Big John's father go?"

"For the moment. But I'm still not satisfied with the old man's story. He's not denying that he was in the vicinity of the old brewery around the time Doc Prentiss says Dunphie died . . . not much point. The publican says the old man was in the Black Swan all evening and was the last to leave. But that's about as much as we can get the wily old beggar to admit to. The extent of his vocabulary appears to be '*Oh aye*,' and that's it!"

"You'll get your answers quicker if you listen to Edwina Charles."

Merton rose. "When she says something worthwhile listening to, I promise you I will. Now, if you don't mind—"

"As you wish," said David, getting to his feet. He smiled. "Okay if I borrow the computer for a couple of minutes?"

Merton eyed him suspiciously. "What for?"

"I'm looking for something."

"I gathered that much. Who?"

"Not *who*, Clive," said David pleasantly. "*What*. . . . A tragic incident—possibly at a children's home in Yorkshire—involving two little orphaned girls, one of whom died, and a man who afterwards made a very sick movie of a little girl in a coffin and another little girl ringing the Devil's Knell by way of penance. This man I mentioned has also probably got a record for sex offences against minors. . . ."

Merton looked at him searchingly, slowly sat down. "Okay," he said. "You win."

"Not me, Clive. Mrs. Charles."

"Who's the man?" Merton sighed.

David shook his head. "It's no use asking me. You know what Edwina Charles is like. She plays by her own set of rules."

Merton stared at him for a moment; then, picking up the telephone receiver, he muttered, "Something tells me we could be in for one or two nasty surprises." He glanced at David and his expression soured. "I suppose Superwoman's got it all worked out what our next move should be!"

"What do you think?" said David. He smiled. "She wants you to go and see a certain nice old lady about a lace-edged, embroidered handkerchief."

Merton looked at him. "Mrs. Frearson?" His eyes widened. "The old lady from the cathedral—St. Anthony's?"

David nodded. "Mrs. Frearson and that particular Lady Chapel handkerchief—which you'll no doubt be as surprised as I was to learn from Mrs. Charles that Mrs. Frearson made specially, many years ago, for a little orphan girl named Mae Holliday—are the bait Mrs. Charles thinks you should use to trap the killer. Mrs. Charles is convinced that the handkerchief is the key to everything. Take her advice, and you'll get your movie-maker served up to you on a plate."

Slowly, Merton put down the telephone receiver. Nothing of what he was thinking—his initial disbelief, then dismay at the apparent importance of Mae Holliday's Lady Chapel handkerchief—registered on his face, but David knew he had been badly fazed by it.

At length, Merton sighed deeply, then shook his head and said, "I don't like it. She . . . the old lady's blind now, isn't she? Eighty-not-out? No, it's too risky. Good God, Dave, what if something went wrong? I can't—*daren't*—take the chance."

"I doubt that Edwina Charles would agree with you there," said David mildly.

"No, she bloody well wouldn't, would she?" snapped Merton. "It's not her head on the chopping-block, is it?" He glared at David; then, muttering irritably to himself, he picked up the receiver again. "I must be mad," he said. "That woman snaps her fingers and everybody jumps. Just what makes her think the handkerchief is so bloody important, anyway? That's what I'd like to know!" he went on muttering to himself. "That old girl must've made hundreds of them. But wouldn't you know it'd be just my luck that the one in Mae Holliday's pocket had to be different from the rest. And wouldn't you just know," he sneered, "that Madame Marvellous would be the one to find out that it was special!" He looked up abruptly and scowled across his desk at David, who was doing his best to keep a straight face. "I'm warning you. If anything goes wrong . . ."

Mrs. Frearson opened the front door of her bungalow. The sun was warm on her face. It was going to be a lovely day for the coach outing; she was so looking forward to it. She only hoped nothing would go wrong again today like last Monday when they should've gone on the outing. . . .

First, Irene Franklin had had to drop out because of her bad fall in the bath-tub a couple of days before, then Margaret Sayer had collapsed, on the very day itself, after that funny business over in that derelict building in the village where she lives, and Helena Winfield had gone over there to help look after her. And then, right at the last minute, some silly, officious inspector had to go and find something wrong with the brakes on the coach, and the tour operator hadn't been able to find a replacement vehicle at such short notice and the outing had had to be postponed. . . .

Mrs. Frearson paused and fumblingly pinned a note to the door, then tapped her way with a slim white stick down a short path to a handrail, one of many in St. Anthony's Village which afforded the partially sighted—and in Mrs. Frearson's case, totally blind—residents greater mobility and independent freedom of movement.

Had Mrs. Frearson followed the handrail to the left of her bungalow, it would have brought her eventually to the superintendent's office. The handrail to the right took her past two other bungalows and into what the residents called "the enchanted garden."

Mrs. Frearson had never seen the enchanted garden, but she knew every plant and shrub in it. The circular and irregular-shaped flower-beds were filled with violet-and-yellow pansies. To her left was a magnolia in full flower and an arbour with wooden bench seating. The arbour was hardly ever used much before morning coffee, and at nine-thirty, when Mrs. Frearson tapped her way past, it was empty.

She was a tall, angular woman who held herself regally erect and walked proudly and with confidence despite her disability. She climbed a steep flight of concrete steps unhesitatingly and then walked on under a Doric-columned pergola towards the miniature oriental bridge over the lily pond.

Pausing momentarily, Mrs. Frearson breathed in the heady scent of the wistaria which twined vigorously up and over the pergola, and turned her head slightly to expose it fully to the pleasing warmth of the sun.

She moved on.

It seemed such a shame—all this beautiful sunshine and fresh air and poor Irene lying in bed in hospital. And all because she simply would *not* slow down and take things steadily and quietly. Everything with Irene (and with a good few others that Mrs. Frearson could think of) was fuss-fuss-rush-rush. It was small wonder there were so many nasty falls, all these broken hips and legs and arms. There were times when a physical handicap wasn't such a bad thing after all, she decided. She mightn't be able to see, but at least all her bones were in good working order and she'd be going on the outing.

She understood there were going to be quite a number of vacant seats on the coach; though her friend Christina, and Christina's daughter Vera, were taking up a couple of the empty places. . . . Barring any more accidents! thought the old lady wryly. That was how it had been right from the start. First one was going, then something happened and that person was out and someone else was in. She was even beginning to wonder if the outing would ever actually take place.

From the lightly wooded copse which bordered the enchanted garden came the sound of a motor-driven chain-saw as men started felling several diseased and dying elms.

The old lady paused on the pretty red-painted wooden footbridge over the lily pond. Behind her, water trickled softly down a stony embankment into the pond, sending out wide ripples in soft waves across the surface of the dark green water. A blackbird sang in a clump of hawthorn somewhere to her right.

She stood with a hand on the side of the bridge listening to the bird's song. It was lovely here, so restful, she thought. But soon she would have to be starting back. Christina and Vera said they would be here at ten.

Mrs. Frearson smiled to herself. Christina had been so surprised about that handkerchief. She was so sure there'd been some mistake.

The blackbird suddenly flew off and Mrs. Frearson turned her head a little as if in anticipation of hearing it start up its song again somewhere else.

Fancy that handkerchief turning up again after all these years. Such a pretty, sunny-natured little girl she was too. Big blue eyes, short, pale golden curls. And to think she was dead. It was really very sad. There had been something about her, though—a hint in that fragile frame of hers that she'd never make old bones.

Mrs. Frearson heard a soft footfall. She listened for a moment, then faced the sound.

"Is that you, Mr. Smith?" she inquired hesitantly.

The superintendent of St. Anthony's Village paused at the bridge and said, "Yes, Mrs. Frearson. You wanted to see me about something?" He glanced at the time, hoped this wasn't going to take long. He felt a little annoyed with the old lady for summoning him and then wandering off from her bungalow and expecting him to come searching for her when he had such a busy morning ahead of him. And he wouldn't be a bit surprised if she couldn't remember why she had wanted to see him. She was growing very forgetful, could recall vividly events which had occurred half a lifetime ago but was becoming increasingly befuddled about the things she'd done as recently as yesterday.

Mrs. Frearson had moved towards him. "I hope you don't mind," she said, pausing when he lightly touched her arm to indicate his proximity to her. "It was such a lovely day, I thought it would be much nicer if we talked out here. I would like your advice about something—that lace handkerchief of poor Miss Holliday's. I was wondering if I should have a word with the police about it."

"Why is that, Mrs. Frearson?" he asked patiently. Poor old thing, he thought. She was missing the limelight, hoping for some of the attention she used to get before she went blind. His tone softened. "I think the police already know it's one of yours."

"Oh yes, I know that, Mr. Smith," she said. "That wasn't what I wanted to tell them. You see, it didn't belong to her. I really am most confused about it. It's so frustrating at times not being able to see. My friend Christina—the one who's coming with us on the outing today—told me that the young woman who was murdered in the Lady Chapel—your young lady—had brown hair and light brown eyes. The little girl I made the handkerchief for—the handkerchief the newspapers said belonged to your young lady—had blue eyes and fair hair. And she died a year later, I heard, of meningitis."

"Well, that explains it," said Jocelyn Smith. "Somehow or other the handkerchief came into Miss Holliday's possession later on."

Mrs. Frearson thought about it. Then, hesitatingly: "Yes, I can see that . . . but it doesn't explain how they both came to have the same name, does it?"

Jocelyn Smith frowned and said, "I'm not sure I understand what you mean, Mrs. Frearson."

"I'm very sorry to have to say this to you, Mr. Smith—I've no doubt that you were very fond of your young lady—but I think she was an impostor." Mrs. Frearson made a small, impatient gesture with her walking-stick. "I only wish I could've seen her face. I'm sure I would've remembered her if she was with the party of little ones that day from Brackenfield House—a children's home in Yorkshire," she explained. "It was closed down a few years later, I was told. There was trouble over some of the young girls in care and a male member of the staff."

Jocelyn Smith again looked at the time. "Well, I don't really know what to say to you, Mrs. Frearson. Quite obviously, this is worrying you, so perhaps you should have a word with the police. I'll phone them as soon as I get back to my office. You'll be out all day. Perhaps you'd like me to make arrangements for them to call and see you sometime tomorrow morning." He paused. Then: "I take it you still want to go on the coach outing today?"

They moved away from the bridge and started slowly back through the enchanted garden.

"Tomorrow will be fine," said Mrs. Frearson. "I wouldn't want to spoil my day: I've been so looking forward to it. I'm sure there'll be an explanation for everything."

They passed leisurely under the pergola.

"I must remember to tell my friend Christina about it," the old lady went on. "She reads a lot of detective stories and is very good at working out puzzles. She might be able to come up with a solution to the mystery."

They stepped out from the pergola into full sunshine, and Jocelyn Smith started down the steps. He looked back when Mrs. Frearson paused.

"If you wouldn't mind assisting me, Mr. Smith," she said. "I do so loathe these concrete steps. I'm always afraid I'm going to miss my footing and slip and fall. And we wouldn't want any more broken bones, would we—?" She smiled.

He returned to her side, but instead of taking her elbow, he hesitated briefly, then stepped suddenly behind her, placed his hands squarely on her back . . .

Someone shouted.

Jocelyn Smith momentarily froze, then looked quickly round. Two men were running swiftly towards him. He saw immediately what had happened. He had been tricked. Mrs. Frearson had lured him out here and those men—plainclothes police officers, he realised—had been shadowing her every step of the way, waiting for him to do precisely this, to try and kill her.

He pushed the old lady roughly aside, ignored the calls to him to remain where he was, and raced down the steps two at a time. He left the path and tore across the lawn, swerving abruptly when a uniformed police officer suddenly loomed up out of the shrubbery ahead of him. He headed for the copse where the tree-felling was in progress.

More uniformed police officers appeared, some running, others waving their arms. There was a lot of shouting, a terrible creaking, groaning noise.

Jocelyn Smith looked up, saw the big tree that was about to fall.

He turned, started to run back, away from it, felt a sudden rush of air, and then it was all around him like a giant clawing octopus.

He struggled helplessly to free himself from a tangle of branches and leaves, thought for a moment that he was going to be all right. He definitely hadn't been hurt, couldn't feel any pain. Then, all of a sudden, he saw the thick branch suspended above his head, heard it groan and creak, then crack. He struggled frantically to free his legs and roll clear, but he couldn't move. He was pinned fast by his ankles to the ground.

Mrs. Frearson heard his hoarse cry, and she turned to Chief Superintendent Merton, who was standing quietly at her side, and asked, "Was that Mr. Smith?"

Merton said it was.

"A tree fell on him," she said matter-of-factly.

"I'm afraid so," said Merton, his gaze focused on the distant scene. "He ran straight into its path. There was nothing anyone could do."

She sighed softly. "Such a nice man," she said. "You're sure about him?"

"Quite sure," said Merton absently.

She said nothing for a moment. Then, with a small sigh: "I didn't think anything was going to happen. He took it all so calmly, and I didn't want to disappoint you—that's if he really was the man you were after—so I said to myself, 'All or nothing, Ethel, my girl,' and I told him I was going to tell my friend Christina what I knew about his girl-friend. That should do the trick, I thought. I mean, he couldn't have me babbling like a brook all over the place about his young lady being an impostor, could he? If he was really guilty of something, that is. And if he was innocent, then nothing would happen, would it? He would simply escort me back to my bungalow and then telephone you like he said and leave it all for you to sort out."

Keeping an eye on the efforts of his men to extricate Jocelyn Smith from the wreckage of the fallen tree, the Chief Superintendent said, "Once the press gets hold of the story, we—the police—are bound to be censured for what we've done here this morning to trap Mr. Smith into betraying himself." He paused and looked at the old lady gravely. "While I feel our actions are justifiable in the circumstances, they were nevertheless most unorthodox. You took a very great risk, you know."

"Fortunately," she said with a solemn smile, "I couldn't see it."

CHAPTER 20

Jean Sayer switched her gaze from her husband to Mrs. Charles as the latter wheeled in the afternoon-tea trolley. The comment which Jean had been about to make to David she directed now to the clairvoyante instead.

"The village store was buzzing with talk about Jocelyn Smith this morning while I was in there, but nobody seemed to know for sure what's really happened. And David and I haven't, of course, been able to talk much about it because of Aunt Margaret. The last thing we wanted was for her to get over-excited again," Jean went on to explain. "Our means of communication over the past couple of days has been largely by hand signals behind her back. The old lady's got ears and eyes on her like a hawk when you don't want her to know what you're talking about."

Jean looked back at her husband. "Is it true that Jocelyn Smith's in hospital, dying?"

"He's in a deep coma," David replied. "The doctors don't really expect him to come round: he got a pretty vicious crack on the skull from the broken bough of the tree that crashed down all around him. But—" he shrugged "—who knows. He could surprise us all. He's survived worse things in the past."

David looked at Mrs. Charles. "Merton said Mrs. Frearson was really quite superb. I gather she enjoyed every moment of the part she played in helping to trap Smith. And she asked me to invite you over for tea with her one Sunday afternoon. She wants to thank you personally for thinking she was up to it and not treating her like she claimed most people tend to nowadays—as if being old and blind with it automatically means she's senile too and going through a second childhood," he finished with a smile.

Jean widened her eyes at the clairvoyante. "Someone said Tilly Cockburn introduced Miss Holliday to Mr. Smith sometime last year; but then just as I was leaving the store this morning, I overheard someone else saying that he'd known Miss Holliday since she was a little girl. They can't both be right."

Mrs. Charles passed Jean a cup of tea and a slice of her own special home-made chocolate cake. Then she said, "The police have now discovered that Mae Holliday—the woman we in the village knew as Mae Holliday—spent the latter part of her childhood in a children's home in West Yorkshire where Jocelyn Smith was employed, first as a caretaker, then later on in a secretarial capacity. At fourteen, she ran away from the home, completely disappeared. The police were notified at the time, but she was never traced. She became just another statistic, one of the hundreds of young people who go missing every year and are never heard of again.

"For approximately four years prior to her disappearance," the clairvoyante went on after serving David with tea and cake, "ever since she was ten years old, Jocelyn Smith had subjected her to terrible mental torment over a tragic incident which had occurred at the home. Finally, she broke down under the strain, and that was when she ran away."

"Yes," said Jean, nodding, "I heard that she was suffering from amnesia and didn't know who she was. What was her real name?"

"Raylene Phillips," David replied. "She was taken permanently into care on the recommendation of her welfare officer when she was seven years old. Her father was dead and her mother had maltreated her since birth. She was fostered out unsuccessfully several times, then over the next three years, she was shunted from one children's home to another until eventually, when she was ten, she was placed in a home for problem children—those like herself who, after having endured years of quite terrible physical abuse, had become hostile and aggressive, unmanageable. And in her case, vicious and spiteful with it, particularly towards another little girl who'd lived at the children's home since she was a few hours old and was a favourite with all the staff. The other child's name was Mae Holliday. She'd been found, quite literally, on the home's front doorstep by Smith, the caretaker/handyman, who suggested naming her after the May Spring Bank Holiday, the day she'd been abandoned.

"There was even a rumour—this was when the police failed to trace the mother," David continued, "that the child was Smith's: he'd got some young local girl into trouble, delivered the child himself, then left it where he could find it and see that it was properly cared for. The child was never considered for adoption because of her poor health. Neither was she moved from that home to another more suitable one because of her close attachment to the staff there. She was a delicate child, never really recovered from her bad start in life. Then, when she was eight, a flu epidemic swept through the home and she became gravely ill. However, she pulled through—or she was making a good recovery—and as a sort of get-well present, Smith gave her an old copy of a magazine about movie stars. She was mad about the cinema and film stars and was always begging the staff to help her to write away for pictures of her favourite actors and actresses.

"Anyway—" David sighed "—Raylene Phillips, who was jealous of all the attention this other child received from the staff, and Smith in particular, took the magazine away from her, and during their squabble about it, Raylene struck little Mae on the back of her head, behind her right ear, with a cricket bat. Nothing happened for a few days, then little Mae complained of an ache in her right ear. An abscess formed and eventually meningitis was diagnosed, from which she never recovered.

"Naturally, everyone at the home was shattered when she died, particularly Smith, and no doubt wrongly, Raylene was sent to Coventry—more or less shunned by the staff and all the other children. Smith, who possibly had an even greater attachment to the dead child (if he was really her father as had once been rumoured), went one step further. He made a home-movie with Raylene in the two leading roles. He was always a bit of an oddball, something of a religious freak. He'd tried and abandoned just about every religious faith known to mankind in his search for one that suited his own particular beliefs, including the occult. He was even a Druid priest for a time. Some years later, when it was the fashionable thing to do, he became fascinated with the religions of the Orient, which he'd visited originally as a Christian missionary. He abandoned this work after a while and entered various Buddhist monasteries, first in India, then afterwards in Japan, where he became proficient in the martial arts. And, incidentally, while he was doing missionary work in India, he almost died of smallpox.

"But all of this came much later, after he'd been dismissed from the children's home," David went on. "Smith had been warned more than once about taking young girls into his—the caretaker's—flat while his wife was out, and he was ultimately dismissed for misconduct with one of the thirteen-year-olds in care. By this time, though, he'd been promoted to a secretarial job within the home. The new caretaker found Smith and the girl together, both only partly clad, in one of the bedrooms, and he reported the matter. This all happened after Raylene had run away.

"She took very little with her when she left: a purse made in the shape of a dog, which her real mother had given her, some money she'd stolen from the superintendent's office, the filmstar magazine she'd taken from little Mae, a lace-edged handkerchief of Mae's—a memento of a visit to Gidding Cathedral which Raylene was known to have coveted because it was different from everyone else's—and the home-movie Smith had made of her—"

Jean interrupted. "The reel of film the police found in Miss Holliday's skirt-pocket?"

Nodding, David said, "Which showed Raylene ringing the Devil's Knell as an act of penance for having caused Mae's death—murdered her, Smith probably felt."

Jean looked at Mrs. Charles and asked, "How did you discover that it wasn't a black magic ritual?"

Mrs. Charles said, "The police don't really know that for certain yet. They will have to talk to Jocelyn Smith about it later—that's if he ever comes round. Cyril—my brother—pointed out the possibility that it mightn't have anything to do with witchcraft."

The clairvoyante smiled at the look on Jean's face. "Yes, I was surprised too. Though I shouldn't have been. Cyril was educated by the Church—he was a boy soprano—and if our mother had had her way, he would've made a career of singing."

"I'll be surprised if he's wrong about that film," said David. "So will Merton—much and all as he'd grudge having to admit it . . . just as he loathed admitting that you were probably right and Smith had once held the film over Raylene-known-as-Mae's head, so to speak."

"What made her choose Gidding, of all places?" asked Jean. "I mean, after she ran away."

Mrs. Charles said, "She went there once as a child to a holiday camp with a party of other children from the home, which included the real Mae Holliday; and while she, Raylene, probably had no idea what brought her to Gidding, I think it could've been the subconscious remembrance of that holiday—the only holiday, the police have discovered after talking to former employees of the home, she'd apparently ever been on—which eventually directed her footsteps there. Though not immediately. There's a gap of two years in her life which no one can account for, when she obviously drifted from place to place, living rough—stealing whenever necessary. She might even have found herself in Gidding again one day purely by chance."

"She honestly didn't know who she really was when she came here and asked you to read the cards for her?" Jean asked the clairvoyante.

"No," replied Mrs. Charles. "But it was slowly coming back to her. She started to remember the day Jocelyn Smith called into the post-office stores seeking directions to someone's house."

Jean asked, "Is this where Tilly comes in?"

The clairvoyante nodded. "Tilly couldn't help him, so she called across the store to Miss Holliday."

"And he recognised her?" asked Jean, wide-eyed.

"No," said David. "At least we don't think so, not right away. The police have talked to Tilly about what happened that day, and she says that as far as she can remember, it wasn't until she called out again to Miss Holliday, and this time used her first name, that Smith seemed interested. But that's only with hindsight, I might add. Apparently, he then moved up to the post-office counter to continue the conversation with Miss Holliday personally and presumably take a closer look at the woman whose name recalled so many disturbing memories."

"Of the little girl who'd died?" Jean looked at Mrs. Charles, who shook her head and said:

"No, I would think he was well and truly over that. What worried him now was the movie he'd made of Raylene Phillips ringing the Devil's Knell. She'd taken it with her when she'd run away from the home, and it would've been natural to assume that she'd kept it. Their roles were now, in effect, reversed. Whereas for years he'd held that film over her head for the part he and everyone else at the home had blamed her for playing in little Mae's death, she was now in a position to hold it over him. She could ruin him, destroy everything he'd achieved. He couldn't let that happen, not after his run of bad luck: first redundancy, then being unable to find work—partly because of his age, and partly because of poor health, a stroke —then landing a job through the Church, and finally, just when everything was going along nicely, losing his wife." The clairvoyante smiled wryly. "If that movie he'd made ever came to light, so might the rest of his dubious career, his weakness for little girls, and his past decidedly unorthodox religious practices."

"The Church didn't uncover any of it when they took him on?" asked Jean.

"No," said David. "After he was dismissed from the children's home, he and his wife parted for a time—this was when he went out to India—then when he became disenchanted with the various Eastern philosophies he'd experimented with there, and afterwards in Japan, he returned home, there was a reconciliation with his wife, and together they drifted all over the place, from one town to another, before finally finishing up in Gidding, where Mrs. Smith was born and still had some family ties. There he got work as a personnel officer with a local engineering firm, which went bust a few years ago. That was when he was made redundant. He got that job on the strength of a previous one, and he got the one with St. Anthony's Village on the strength of the one with the local company. Nobody bothered to go any further back. The Church certainly didn't. He had glowing testimonials from his previous employers, the engineering firm, for whom he had worked for over eight years; and as a personnel officer, he had just the right kind of background and training for the post they sought to fill.

"However, when fate eventually brought him here to the village, Mae Holliday—the postmistress—didn't recognise him. It was eighteen years since they'd last met. He was in his thirties then, blond, reasonably good-looking, and was known as Eddie, short for Edward. Jocelyn is his middle name. He started using Jocelyn after his dismissal from the home, one would assume in the hope that by so doing, his questionable past would be less easy to trace. A balding, white-haired old man named Jocelyn Smith was a complete stranger to her. Neither did his surname trigger off any positive past remembrance of him. The name was too common for that."

David looked at Mrs. Charles, who nodded and said, "But nevertheless, something obviously clicked in the back of her mind without her actually being aware of it. And from that day on, approximately eighteen months ago, little by little, the fact that she'd known him when she was a child slowly bubbled to the surface of her consciousness.

"Mr. North—Stan North, our local weather expert," the clairvoyante went on, "told me that he came upon them one day out in the countryside, and that unknown to them, he over-heard snatches of their conversation with one another. She called Jocelyn Smith 'Mr. Smith.' Stan North thought she was merely being playful, kittenish. I personally doubt it. I would think that this was how she always addressed him . . . Be-cause subconsciously she remembered that to her—as a child—he was *Mr.* Smith. He was over twenty years older than she was, and it would've therefore been very unlikely that she, a young child, would've used his first name. She probably wasn't even aware—as an adult now, that is—that she was addressing him so formally."

Jean looked bemused. "I wonder what he made of it all."

The clairvoyante said, "To begin with, I would imagine he was exceedingly puzzled. Relieved, no doubt, when he realised that she was suffering from loss of memory. It gave him time to work out a way to get hold of the reel of film, or to discover whether it was still in existence, without alerting her as to who he was. Ultimately, it would seem that he came to the conclu-sion that his best bet was to marry her."

"So why kill her?" asked Jean.

The clairvoyante smiled faintly. "His solution became his undoing. He completely forgot that while he knew who our village postmistress really was, she didn't. It was a problem for her, not for him, so he didn't foresee the difficulties a proposal of marriage would entail for someone like her, for anyone who had been living a lie. And, I might say, quite happily and con-tentedly in her case. I think there's every possibility that she would've lived out the remainder of her life here in the village as its postmistress, as Miss Dunphie had before her, if Jocelyn Smith hadn't disturbed the cobwebs in the back of her mind and made her discontented.

"However, as I was saying, Miss Holliday had to know who she really was before she could accept anybody's marriage proposal—for all she knew, she might already be married!—so she came to me and asked me to help her to unlock the past."

Mrs. Charles paused. Then, meditatively: "I'm not sure how Jocelyn Smith found out she came to see me—possibly she herself told him, though it wouldn't seem very likely. But somehow he discovered that she'd been here and talked to me, and I think he feared the worst and panicked. The police know that an anonymous caller, a man (Jocelyn Smith, we must now assume), phoned Arthur Dunphie's digs last Saturday week and left a message with the landlady requesting Arthur to meet him outside The Brewery after closing time at the Black Swan that night; and I would think much the same thing happened with Miss Holliday, only in her case, Jocelyn Smith would've almost certainly spoken to her direct over the phone, disguising his voice. And I've no doubt that the bait he used in this instance, which she would've found irresistible, was that he could give her information about herself, her past.

"I'm quite sure it goes without saying that she was instructed to take the reel of film with her when she went to meet her mysterious phone caller in the Lady Chapel that Thursday, the day following her visit to me," the clairvoyante continued. "And it had to be a Thursday because that was market-day in Gidding, and Big John Little, whom Jocelyn Smith planned to frame for her murder, would be there selling his bundles of withies.

"Miss Holliday might've finally remembered who Jocelyn Smith really was before he killed her—only he could tell us that, should he recover from his head injuries. But I personally think she did." Mrs. Charles paused. Then, pensively: "It's been suggested that Jocelyn Smith might've unlocked the Lady Chapel door earlier in the morning. . . . I don't think so. I prefer to think that he knocked on the door, that this was prearranged between them, and that when she unlocked it and saw him standing there, everything slotted into place. Vera Markham—the woman who'd fallen asleep in the church while she was waiting to use the Lady Chapel—dreamt that a man was threatening her (Mrs. Markham) about something which she was keeping in her possession; but I would be more inclined to think that she'd subconsciously heard Jocelyn Smith threaten Miss Holliday about the film when she wouldn't hand it over to him. Mrs. Markham simply wove this into her dream. I'm also convinced that she unwittingly heard Jocelyn Smith knocking on the chapel door and that similarly, she later found a suitable spot for this in her dream."

The clairvoyante went on: "Miss Holliday was an intelligent woman; she would've quickly perceived that her life was now in mortal danger because of the reel of film she'd kept. I also think she would've realised that she might be able to save herself if she lied and said she hadn't brought it along with her. She was certainly shrewd enough not to carry it about in her handbag in case something went wrong when she met her mysterious male caller and he didn't live up to his part of their bargain. Jocelyn Smith gambled that she was bluffing. He killed her with a blow to the back of the head and left her lying on the altar step stabbed with a withy stake. Then he went through her handbag, but he couldn't find the film. It never occurred to him to look in the concealed pocket of his victim's skirt—he probably wasn't even aware of its existence. And in any event, I would say that it was about now that Mrs. Markham woke up and decided she couldn't wait any longer. He heard her collecting her things together, and he quickly left through the Lady Chapel door, taking the key with him and using it to lock up behind him. He crossed the cloisters, then he went down the alley-way which debouches into Monks Lane. From there he proceeded towards the square. . . ."

David took up the narrative. "By which time Mrs. Markham had made her gruesome discovery in the Lady Chapel and reached the bus-stop and fainted. She came round and said she'd seen a woman lying dead, murdered, in the Lady Chapel. There was apparently some sort of conference about what should be done next, then somebody suggested that it might be an idea to check first before calling the police or an ambulance, and so a posse of about fifteen people, by this time, set off for the cathedral."

"With Jocelyn Smith?" asked Jean.

David nodded. "Merton's chaps have since found two people from the bus-stop posse who remember seeing a man amongst them answering to Smith's description. And in the confusion in the Lady Chapel—a couple of women had hysterics, another collapsed with a heart attack—he quickly popped the key back in the door where it belonged. Since deciding, for purely practical reasons this time, that the Anglican faith might be the one for him after all, he'd been steadily working his way up in the Church—St. Anthony's, that is. He was on the council—a warden—so he knew all about the door to the Lady Chapel. And then after he'd replaced the key, he simply drifted away. More or less unnoticed."

"What a despicable thing to do, trying to pin the murder on Big John Little by staking Miss Holliday through the chest with one of his withies," said Jean disgustedly.

"Yes," agreed David. "But you've got to admit that it was good thinking on his part. He must've slipped into the village the night before while Big John and his dad were down at the Black Swan and helped himself to what he needed. The withy shed is never locked up. It wouldn't make much difference if it were: you can walk straight through some of the gaps in the walls! I daresay Smith even borrowed Big John's special tools to sharpen the withy to a point." David grinned at his wife. "Just let it be a lesson to you never to get drunk and threaten to kill someone you don't like where everyone can hear you."

"I'll try to remember, sir," said Jean, mock-seriously. She hesitated, frowned.

"What is it?" her husband asked.

She hesitated again. Then, smiling quickly at Mrs. Charles, she said, "I was simply wondering how you found out that it was Jocelyn Smith who'd killed Miss Holliday."

The clairvoyante watched a faint blush colour the other woman's face. Jean had been going to say something else and had changed her mind, thought better of it.

Mrs. Charles smiled. "I simply put two and two together— something Miss Holliday said to me, with something Jocelyn Smith said—and went on from there."

David listened with particular interest. It was a question the clairvoyante had hitherto avoided giving a direct answer to, and he had assumed that her reluctance to divulge the exact source of her information on Smith indicated that she had used her powers of clairvoyance to nail him and that she had not wished to admit it and thereby subject herself to police ridicule. Merton, David smiled to himself, hated clairvoyants, would've torn her to shreds (metaphorically speaking, that is) if she'd tried to tell him she'd seen it all in the crystal ball!

Jean was querying the clairvoyante about what it was that had been said to her which had aroused her suspicions. . . .

Mrs. Charles replied, "Miss Holliday used the expression, 'Needs must when the Devil drives.' It was something, she told me, she remembered from the past. Someone used to say it to her a long while ago. Possibly Agatha Dunphie, I thought," admitted the clairvoyante with a faint shrug. "The sentiment expressed by those few words quoted by Miss Holliday was certainly Miss Dunphie's brand of philosophy. And I never thought any more about it. Not even when Jocelyn Smith made his slip—in the form of a jest—and in so doing, as good as told me that he was the dominant male figure in Miss Holliday's past who'd obviously used that phrase so frequently in her presence when she was a child that it had become cemented in her memory.

"It wasn't until after Cyril had pointed out that I might be wrong about the content of the Mae Holliday movie and I started to reflect on all the other mistakes that had been made, individually—" she smiled "—and collectively as a result of that one particular mistake—if it were a mistake—that I suddenly found myself thinking about my conversation with Jocelyn Smith, the comment he'd made about mistakes, errors. He said he didn't believe there were any, they were all part of the Creator's plan . . . something along those lines. And then I remembered what he'd said to me in reply to my query concerning his motives for wishing to marry Miss Holliday.

"And, I might add," she put in quickly with another smile, "I was not quite so blunt as that; or I'd tried not to be, though he did see through me. He, however, took it all in good part, and as I've said, jokingly replied, in the words of the Countess of Rousillon from—ironically enough—*All's Well that Ends*

Well, 'Tell me thy reason why thou wilt marry.' And then, quoting the reply of the Clown, to whom the Countess was speaking: 'My poor body, madam, requires it: I am driven on by the flesh. . . .'

"He then went on to give me a proper answer to my question. But had he finished the Clown's dialogue from that section of the play, he would've added, after 'I am driven on by the flesh', 'and he must needs go that the Devil drives.' Or in modern parlance, as Miss Holliday had said to me—and Jocelyn Smith, I later began to suspect, habitually used to say to her, and probably to others—'Needs must when the Devil drives!'"

David gave a short, dry laugh. "Well, the Devil—and Smith —certainly drove us. And no one can say they didn't lead us a fine old dance while they were about it. All the way!"

"Yes," said the clairvoyante quietly. "I thought so too."

CHAPTER 21

David and Jean were driving home when Jean made her confession.

"You know when you asked me what was wrong . . ." she began pensively. "Just before we left Mrs. Charles?"

Her husband nodded.

"Well, it was what you'd just said about the dangers of getting drunk and talking too much. I very nearly let the cat out of the bag about your aunt."

"How do you mean?"

"That's how Jocelyn Smith found out that Miss Holliday had gone to see Mrs. Charles: your aunt told Helena Winfield, and Helena Winfield told Jocelyn Smith. They thought they were saving him from a fate worse than death. That was if he really was going to marry Miss Holliday."

David took his eyes momentarily off the road and looked at his wife. It was a while before he spoke.

"You know what you're saying, don't you?" he said quietly.

"Yes," she said. "Your aunt killed Miss Holliday, and poor Big John. With her tongue."

And Arthur Dunphie made it a hat trick, thought David.

Aunt Margaret was in the post-office stores that Saturday morning when Dunphie called in, and she either overheard him telling Tilly that he was going to consult his solicitor about the reel of movie-film—in the hope that it would help him to prove that Mae Holliday was a witch and had used witchcraft on his aunt, and he could then overturn his aunt's will—or Tilly discussed his plans with Aunt Margaret after he had left. . . .

And Aunt Margaret had told Helena Winfield, and Helena Winfield had told Jocelyn Smith!

Which had left Smith with no alternative. He had to kill Arthur Dunphie too. He couldn't have Dunphie stirring things up about that film. The more fuss that was made about it, the greater the risk of its true meaning and purpose coming to light.

It was vital to Smith that everyone believed, and continued to believe, that Mae Holliday was a witch, involved with a local coven, and that the film was part and parcel of that side of her life. So he lured Dunphie over to the village late at night with, as Dunphie's landlady had told the police, the promise that he was about to hear something to his advantage. Smith killed him, then set about making it look as though Dunphie had stumbled on the local witches' coven and had had to be silenced.

And Smith, having once dabbled in the occult, knew just enough about pentacles and the like to make this theory seem feasible. Keys to Rose Cottage and the post-office stores were found on Dunphie by the police, and there was no doubt in David's mind that Smith had "borrowed" them, that it was he, and not Dunphie, who had helped himself to the clock in the store. Though for reasons far removed from those Dunphie had had in mind, thought David grimly. Agatha Dunphie's old railway clock had provided Smith with an indisputable link with the Mae Holliday movie, a final macabre touch.

Jean sighed softly. "You were right about your aunt that day," she said as David turned the car on to their drive and she began to unfasten her safety-belt. "She really is a dangerous old woman."

"Yes," he agreed. And his blood ran cold.

Miss Sayer was feeling much better, well enough to have spent the past hour sitting in the bay window with her opera-glasses, watching the road.

David and Jean had left Mrs. Charles's bungalow fifteen minutes ago, that fool Stan North was poking about in the stretch of pasture-land beyond Mr. Curry's place, gradually working his way up to the road, and the Dixons were in their front garden pruning the roses. Nothing much else of interest was going on. . . .

Miss Sayer was bored, fed up with being treated like a child, everybody creeping around whispering, "Ssh, she'll hear you; don't upset her!"

The old lady's eyes suddenly narrowed and she leaned quickly forward.

That was a police car!

She watched the car draw up outside Mr. Curry's cottage. Two uniformed police officers got out, knocked on Mr. Curry's door, spoke to him for a moment or two, and then everybody disappeared indoors.

Miss Sayer kept the glasses to her eyes, waited.

Five minutes later, the policemen reappeared, accompanied by Mr. Curry, and went into the greenhouse. They weren't out there for more than a minute, just long enough to collect a plant. Then all three men came out and got into the police car and drove off.

Mr. and Mrs. Dixon, the middle-aged couple who lived opposite Mr. Curry, strolled casually over to talk to Stan North, who was currently occupied in the hedgerow bordering the other side of the road.

Miss Sayer dropped the glasses down the side of her chair and went to get her coat. The evening had turned cool with a hint of rain, and she didn't want to add a chill to all her other problems.

Stan North smiled to himself as he saw her bearing down on him. The Dixons had returned to their roses.

"Evening, Miss Sayer," he said pleasantly. "Nice to see you up and about again."

"Where's that Rafe Curry gone?" she panted breathlessly.

He turned his head and gazed intently along the road. Then, peering myopically at a tiny insect which was crawling across the delicate lacy remnants of a dead leaf: "Oh, he's helping the police with their inquiries."

"Inquiries into what?"

"Those plants he grows out back in his greenhouse. They're going to fetch someone over from Customs and Excise to put a seal on the door."

The old lady stared at him. Since when was it against the law for a man to grow a few harmless pot plants in his own greenhouse?

"You must think I'm a fool, Stan North!" she snorted, and marched off back home.

ABOUT THE AUTHOR

MIGNON WARNER was born in Australia, but now lives in England with her husband, whom she assists in the invention, design and manufacture of magic apparatus. She spends most of her free time pursuing her interest in psychic research and the occult. Her previous novels about the clairvoyant Mrs. Charles include THE GIRL WHO WAS CLAIRVOYANT, DEATH IN TIME and THE TAROT MURDERS.